SHAL ACADEMY

THE WHISPERING WALLS

First published in the UK in 2024 by Usborne Publishing Limited., Usborne House, 83-85 Saffron Hill, London EC1N 8RT, England, usborne.com

Usborne Verlag, Usborne Publishing Limited., Prüfeninger Str. 20, 93049 Regensburg, Deutschland, VK Nr. 17560

Text copyright © Phil Hickes, 2024

A CIP catalogue record for this book is available from the British Library.

JFMAMJJASON /23 ISBN 9781805314905 9396/1

Printed and bound using 100% renewable electricity by CPI Group (UK) Ltd, CR0 4YY

MIX
Paper | Supporting
responsible forestry
FSC® C171272

SHADOWHALL ACADEMY

THE WHISPERING WALLS

Phil Hickes

USBORNE

Chapter 1

Suffolk, England, September 1987

Lilian Jones sat in the back of her dad's Ford Escort and watched her old life slowly disappear. Everything she had thought set in stone was crumbling away. Her home. Her friends. Her treasured bedroom in the attic of their cosy house, where all her precious things were neatly laid out. Her seashell collection, ordered in size from large to small. Her colour coded jars of marbles, which she never actually played with, but simply enjoyed looking at. Her bookshelf, the authors arranged in alphabetical order, just like in a library. All this and more was now a hundred miles behind her. On the radio, Madonna was urging everybody to *get into the groove*, but Lilian wasn't in the mood right now.

"Could you change the station, Dad?" Lilian asked.

"Everything okay back there?" her dad asked, reaching for the tuner.

"Fine thanks," Lilian's little sister Susan said, her voice happy and light, like the first day of spring.

"I was asking Lilian," their dad said. "I know you're alright, Susan, you're not the one starting a new school."

"Oh, sorry, Dad," Susan said, before throwing a guilty look in Lilian's direction. "Sorry, Lilian."

"Don't worry, Susan, it's me that's about to get eaten alive," Lilian said. "Not you."

Lilian hadn't meant to sound so harsh and didn't like seeing the hurt expression on Susan's face. It was only because she was struggling to keep her own emotions concealed. It felt as if any minute all her features might slowly start to slide down her face, like melting snow. But she wasn't about to do that in front of her little sister. Susan always looked to her for approval and Lilian was happy to supply it. It felt good to be looked up to. Neither did she want her dad to know that she was scared and nervous.

Lilian's mother had gone to boarding school and always wanted Lilian to do the same. Then, Shadowhall Academy had caught her mum's eye. Lilian immediately had her doubts. Just because her mum had *had the most amazing time ever*, didn't guarantee she would, too. And what about her friends, Joey and Sarah, who she went exploring on the beach with, finding more seashells to add to her collection? But then her parents had shown her a brochure for the academy and she couldn't help but feel her heart leap a little. The school was huge, with sloping lawns, its great Gothic turrets silhouetted against the skyline like something from another time. It had gleaming wood-panelled classrooms. A gigantic library. A majestic dining hall. Sports fields. Dormitories. An impressive cast of immaculately educated teachers. Everything perfectly organized, just like Lilian liked it. She'd always wanted to go somewhere exciting and different – well, here was her chance. And so, after a little resistance, she'd agreed to give it a go.

Yet thinking about something was different from actually doing it. And for the first time in her life, Lilian had to admit that maybe she wasn't quite as adventurous as she imagined herself to be. Shadowhall opened its doors to students as young as eight, so many of the other girls had already been there for years. Maybe they would all be so close that it would be impossible for Lilian to make friends? She wondered if perhaps it would have been safer to have stayed in her bedroom, pottering about with seashells. Because right at this moment, she was fighting the urge to beg her dad to turn the car around and take her home.

Too late now.

Her dad was slowing down, and before long, the wide, grey, monotonous motorway had been replaced by leafy country lanes. Lilian sighed and glanced over the fields. The trees had begun to change out of their green summer uniforms into the red, gold and oranges of autumn.

"I love autumn," Susan said. "It's so colourful."

"That's because everything's dying," Lilian said.

"Oh, Lilian, don't ever change," her dad said.

"Well, it's true," Lilian said. "Those are the signs of decomposition and death. There's no point pretending otherwise."

"I just like the colours," Susan sniffed. "They're beautiful."

"Are you sure you're alright, Lilian?" her dad asked again. "I know you're nervous but that's fine. Starting a new school, away from home, is a big deal, and what you're feeling is totally normal."

How did her dad know? Lilian thought she'd done a good job of putting a brave face on things. Obviously not.

"I'm fine, Dad, honestly," Lilian lied again. "I just want to get there."

"Well, won't be long now. Hang in there."

Lilian slid back in her seat, aware that her sister kept glancing over at her, as if she wanted to say something but wasn't sure whether she would get her head bitten off again. Lilian hoped she would stay quiet. Although her sister was only three years younger, Lilian still thought of Susan as like a teddy bear – all soft, blonde fur, made from love and care and kindness. At this precise moment, if her sister said anything nice, Lilian feared she wouldn't be able to fight the tears any longer. Her carefully built dam would burst.

Yet as her dad had promised, it wasn't long before the car began to climb up a hill and they came to an impressive set of tall, wrought-iron gates. Right on top, made from the same blackened iron, was a ferocious-looking creature growling at the outside world. While Lilian's dad got out to ring the bell, Lilian studied the creature.

"Is that a *dog* with two heads?" Susan asked.

"I think it's a gargoyle," Lilian corrected, suppressing a tiny shudder.

"It's terrifying," Susan said, with a horrified look. "Why would you put that on the gates of a school?"

"Because it wasn't always a school," Lilian said. "It was someone's house before that. It said so in the brochure."

"I wouldn't want one on *my* house."

"I think it's interesting," Lilian said. "Better than a pair of garden gnomes."

"I like garden gnomes," Susan said. "They look after the vegetables and flowers in your garden."

"They eat raw goldfish," Lilian retorted. "Just scoop them out of the pond and munch…bones and all."

"That's not true!"

Thankfully, before Lilian had time to torment her little sister further, their dad had returned and got back into the car as the gates began to slowly swing open. Discussions about murderous garden ornaments were quickly forgotten as they drove slowly through the gates, the turrets of Shadowhall Academy looming in the distance.

"Wow," Susan said. "This place is like a palace."

It was impressive, Lilian had to agree. Much more so in real life than in the brochure. Huge oak trees lined the road, beyond which the fields stretched away towards some woods, the tips of the leaves showing off the golden glow of autumn. There was a small lake, in the middle of which was an island with a strange domed building on it.

Lilian didn't have time to study it further as a group of girls came running past their car, all identically dressed in navy and gold running outfits. They all looked so impressive, like a troop of warriors training for battle. For the first time since they'd set off, Lilian felt her fear replaced by something else. A flutter of excitement. A surge of hope. This place *was* amazing, her sister was right. This was officially the start of an adventure and Lilian had a sense that, just maybe, she had made the right decision.

Her dad brought the car to a halt in front of the main entrance, and even before the engine had died, a tall lady was descending the steps to greet them. Dressed in a smart suit, with her hair tightly pulled back, she wore a stiff smile and had cold, grey eyes. She looked as if she'd been carved from stone.

Lilian's dad climbed out, the two sisters lingering slightly behind him.

"Mr Jones? We spoke on the telephone. I'm Marilyn Strange, headmistress of Shadowhall Academy."

"Pleasure to meet you," Lilian's dad said, stretching out a hand. The woman grasped the tips of his fingers and gave them a hasty shake, as if she was touching a handful of dead fish.

"And hello to you," Ms Strange said, locking her fearsome grey eyes on Susan. "Oh, you're not Lilian, are you?"

"No, I'm Susan. Hello, very nice to—"

"I'm Lilian," Lilian interrupted. Taking a deep breath, she stepped forward and offered her hand. "Pleased to meet you."

"Welcome," Ms Strange said, her eyes narrowing as she appraised Lilian from head to toe. "It's nice to finally meet you, Lilian. I hope you'll be very happy here."

"Thank you," Lilian said. "I'm sure I will."

Lilian wasn't entirely sure this was true. After meeting Ms Strange her stomach felt like a bowlful of jelly. But she thought saying, "Actually, I feel scared sick," probably wasn't appropriate right now.

"Excellent," Ms Strange said. "A positive attitude. That will get you far here, young lady. Just to remind you that while the girls who are already resident here arrived back yesterday, there are going to be other new arrivals starting the autumn term today, too, so you won't be alone. Well, I'll give you a moment to say farewell to your father and sister, then I'll show you to your dormitory."

Saying that, Ms Strange retreated to the top of the steps, clasped her hands and bowed her head, as if not wanting to intrude. It seemed they would be getting straight down to business.

A little self-consciously, Lilian turned to Susan.

"I know the exact position of everything in my bedroom, Susan. And I mean, *everything*."

"I know you do," Susan laughed. "But I don't want to go in your bedroom, so you don't have to worry."

"Bye then."

"See you at Christmas."

They hugged. Lilian felt her sister's hands tighten around her back for a moment. There was a soft breath on the side of her neck. Susan always smelled sweet, like custard and cake. Lilian tightened her grip a little, before pushing her sister away.

"I mean it, no trespassing." Then she turned to her dad. "See you, Dad."

She felt her dad's arms do the same as Susan's, only they held her tighter and for longer.

"I'm proud of you, Lilian," her dad said in a soft voice. "Me *and* your mum. And if you don't like it, you don't have to stay. Just say the word and we'll be up here like a shot to fetch you back."

This was the final straw. Lilian felt a warm tear trickle slowly down her cheek, and quickly wiped it away on her dad's jumper. He smelled of the woody Old Spice aftershave he would splash all over himself in the bathroom.

"Thanks, Dad," she mumbled through a mouthful of wool. "I'll be fine."

"I know you will."

Lilian blinked her eyes clear and turned to gaze up at the intimidating building in front of her. Then her dad handed over her suitcase with both hands, as if its contents were extremely fragile, and gave her a final squeeze on her shoulder.

"Bye, love. Call us when you've settled in, okay?"

Then she was waving goodbye, taking a deep breath, and waiting to see what her new life would bring.

The first thing it brought was a very long and confusing journey through the school – not helped by Ms Strange flinging her arms this way and that as she pointed things out.

"The chemistry lab. The music room. Toilets. Changing rooms. The art studio. The workshop. First aid…"

And on it went, a confusing barrage of rooms and places that Lilian knew she would never remember. It was so much larger than her old school. What was even more distracting was the sea of faces that passed her on the way, the schoolgirls murmuring, "Hello, miss" to Ms Strange before flashing Lilian a quick look, each one sending its own silent message.

Not another new girl.

Ha, you look terrified.

Get out of the way.

I feel sorry for you.

What are you looking at?

It was a bewildering journey, a dizzying succession of narrow corridors that all looked the same, distinguished only by various aromas of talcum powder, bleach, and frying bacon. Lilian began to feel quite light-headed and by the time they'd ascended two sets of stairs she felt ready for a lie-down.

"Now then, I want you to meet Marian Dawson," Ms Strange said. "You'll be sharing a dormitory. She'll show you around and help you find your bearings. Marian has been at Shadowhall for three years now so you're in good hands."

They'd stopped outside an office door. A girl stepped forward and gave Lilian a warm smile. She was smaller than Lilian, who was tall for her age, and had spiky, frizzy black hair which sprouted out in all directions.

"Hello, nice to meet you," Lilian said, feeling a spasm of nerves in her stomach. This was the first girl she'd met at Shadowhall Academy. "I'm Lilian. Lilian Jones."

"Nice to meet you, too, Lilian. I'm Marian. Everyone calls me Maz."

"*Marian*," Ms Strange said, emphasizing her full name, "will show you to your dormitory and help you get acquainted with everyone and everything. In the meantime, if you have any problems, you'll find me here. I shall see you at supper."

And with that Ms Strange swept into her office like a winter breeze.

"What do you think of it so far then?" Marian said as she led Lilian along yet another corridor.

"I'm not sure yet. I've never seen so many girls in one place."

"There are day girls and there are boarders," Marian explained. "Day girls are called that because they live nearby so they go home at night. Us boarders don't get to escape I'm afraid."

Lilian wasn't sure she liked the sound of that, but Marian gave her a smile.

"Okay, we take a left here," she said, leading Lilian up

a wide staircase and down yet another corridor that looked exactly like all the others.

"I don't think I'll ever remember where everything is," Lilian said. "It's so big."

"Oh, you'll get the hang of it soon enough," Marian said. "It's funny. It all feels very small to me now, like being trapped in a snow globe."

Lilian gave Marian a sideways glance.

"What do you mean?"

"Just how something large can start to feel very small after a while. But I'm a goth so don't listen to me; we always look on the dark side of life."

"A goth?"

"Yeah, you know. We like graveyards and bats. Listen to The Cure. Always wear black, at least when we're not made to wear this," she said, gesturing to the uniform, which was navy with gold trim. "We're into anything that's dark and gloomy. That's why I dye my hair black, too, but you have to promise not to tell anyone, because we're not allowed to. There are *rules*, you see. Lots and lots of rules."

Lilian wondered if she might be a goth, too. Her hair was already black, and although she couldn't recall ever having a fondness for graveyards, she had heard of The

Cure, and she did find herself drawn to gloomy thoughts. She had no time to ponder it further though, because Marian had nudged her in the ribs.

"Talking of which, watch out, here comes a vampire."

Chapter 2

Lilian followed Marian's gaze. A small, slender man, dressed in an ill-fitting black suit, shuffled towards them. His head seemed too large for his body and his gait was very odd, Lilian noticed. He walked as if he was trying not to be seen, clinging so close to the wall of the corridor that he would catch his shoulder every few steps and do a funny little twist. His hair was long and rose back from his forehead into a huge dark cloud, as if it had been caught by a gust of wind and then frozen in that position.

"Good afternoon, sir," Marian said, as the man approached.

He darted a nervous glance at them both, his eyes large, watery and pale blue.

"Marian." He paused as he looked again at Lilian, his

small mouth twitching. "I'm terribly sorry, I can't recall your name."

Lilian attempted to put on her friendliest smile, hoping she didn't look like a ventriloquist's dummy.

"Lilian Jones."

"Lilian is new, sir," Marian added. "She just arrived today."

"Ah, that would be why then. Pleasure to meet you, Lilian, I'm Simon Bullen."

"Mr Bullen teaches history," Marian added.

"Hello," Lilian said.

Mr Bullen stared at them both for another uncomfortable few seconds.

"Well, welcome again, Lilian. I'll see you both at supper."

"Thank you," Lilian said, before Mr Bullen continued his strange shuffling dance down the corridor.

"Told you he looked like a vampire," Marian said.

"I thought he looked nervous."

"Because he's out in the daylight, that's why. You'd be nervous too if you thought you might burst into flames and die horribly at any moment."

It was at that moment Lilian decided she and Marian were going to be good friends and the spiky ball of knots and nerves in her stomach began to unravel a little.

"Come on," said Marian, leading Lilian to a grand staircase. "The dorms are right at the top."

The staircases were made of old, stained wood, at the ends of which were matching wooden figures that looked as if they might be lions. There was nothing like this in Lilian's old school. Here, she was beginning to feel rather grand, too. Normally she would only see stuff like this on a guided tour through a stately home, but she lived here now. This was *her* school. The floors were tiled in a black and white pattern and there were large portraits hanging on the walls. The higher they climbed, the narrower the hallways became. They were crooked and winding, the floors cracked and uneven, rising in strange little hills and bumps. It was cold, too. Lilian's fingers began to feel stiff, and she crunched them into the palm of her hand. Eventually, Marian paused outside a door, held out her hand and gave a little bow like a butler.

"After you, ma'am," she said in a pretend posh accent.

Lilian pushed open the door. Her dormitory smelled of furniture polish, but it wasn't unpleasant. It had whitewashed walls, the only decoration a painting of a sad-looking Jesus with a halo. The windows were huge and overlooked the sweeping lawns and the wood and lake beyond. Each one had a giant pair of burgundy velvet curtains which must have stretched ten feet high and weighed a ton. There were four beds in total. Each girl had a small wardrobe and a desk beside their bed. Most alarming, for Lilian, was the lack of privacy. She didn't even have to share a bedroom with her sister, Susan. Now she would be sharing a bedroom with three strangers. This was a situation that she had no experience of, and the prospect made her nervous. Did she snore? Talk in her sleep? She had no idea.

"You can put your stuff in there," Marian said, pointing to the wardrobe next to an unclaimed bed. "The bathrooms are next door but don't go in there without your dressing gown on, they're freezing."

"Is there anywhere warm in this place?"

"No, not really. You sort of get used to being permanently cold."

Lilian placed her suitcase on her new bed and opened it. Her belongings had been packed into neat little squares, all the clothes pressed and folded as if they'd just come new from the shop. Lilian had insisted on doing it herself, despite her mum's offer of help. She liked to be in charge of her own things. In the corner of her suitcase was a small shell, which Lilian had found on the beach in a place called Malmouth. Her parents had taken them there once and this particular shell had been the first in what later became a quite extensive collection.

Just as she was about to place it on the bedside table, she heard the door creak open and a voice called out.

"Hey, Spooky, who's the new shipmate?"

She turned to see a tall girl looking at her with a bemused expression. It made Lilian feel nervous again.

"Her name is Lilian Jones." Marian sighed. "Lilian, this is Serena Khan, the High Queen of Shadowhall. Or at least that's how she sees herself. Her dad drives a Rolls-Royce. Really, she should be at some posh school in Switzerland but her dad didn't fancy shelling out the cash so she ended up here with us."

Serena was as tall as Lilian, with long black hair that flowed over her shoulders like a shining cloak. Her dark eyes glittered with mischief. Serena was beautiful but with a cruel look. Like a jagged mountain peak.

"I can't help it if my papa's loaded," Serena snapped. "And he drives a Bentley, just for the record. Anyway, I see you've been dyeing your hair again, Spooky. I assume Ms Strange gave you special permission?"

This made Marian's already pale face go a little paler.

Lilian had no idea whether this girl was friend or foe. She bowed her head, willing Serena to pass on by. She wanted time to ease her way in before any uncomfortable encounters presented themselves. But to her dismay, she heard footsteps and a shadow fell across the bed. Serena sniffed very loudly.

"That's a nice seashell," she said. "Can I have it?"

Lilian took a deep breath. It appeared that this was to be her first test. And she needed to get safely through it.

"No, sorry, it's like my lucky charm."

Serena stretched out a hand and wiggled her fingers on the edge of Lilian's case.

"Well, now it can be my lucky charm, can't it?"

Lilian felt her face flush. Turning, she locked eyes with Serena.

"Have you ever heard of the vagus nerve?"

Serena frowned.

"The what?"

"The vagus nerve," Lilian continued. "You see, if somebody presses their knuckle on a certain point in your neck, it hits the vagus nerve and can cause temporary blindness, or even unconsciousness. My father showed me how to do it once."

This was a lie. Lilian had only read about it in a book. But when she saw Serena's eyes widen and her mouth fall open, she felt relieved that she'd prepared in advance.

24

Her dad had cautioned her that sometimes schools came with bullies and so she'd determined to have something up her sleeve. A strategy. Something that might at least make someone think she was tougher than she looked.

"Alright, new girl, keep your wig on," Serena said. "I was only asking."

Then Serena flounced away, pausing to flick Marian's hair as she passed, almost like a consolation prize.

"Well, Maz," Serena said, flopping down on her bed and picking up a Sony Walkman. "It seems our new friend has a problem with sharing things."

"I didn't mean that…" Lilian began, but Serena placed her headphones on, switched the play button, and the sound of a tinny drumbeat filled the room.

"Ignore her," Marian said. "She's just trying to get the measure of you, she does it all the time."

Unsure if she'd overreacted, Lilian silently returned to her unpacking. She knew that it was important to make friends. Now she might have made an enemy on her very first day. Marian was impressed though.

"I've never seen anyone put Serena in her place so quickly," she whispered, her eyes shining with glee as she came to sit on the end of Lilian's bed. "And Serena's not scared of anything except heights."

"She's scared of heights?"

"Absolutely petrified. Says she can't go anywhere high up without feeling terrified and sick. Anyway, was that true about the *vaguest verve* thing?"

"Vagus nerve," Lilian corrected. "Yes it's true, but I have no idea how to do it."

"Ha!" Marian exclaimed. "Even better! I think that's two things she's terrified of now – heights and you."

Lilian didn't want Serena to be terrified of her.

But she didn't mind her being a little wary.

Supper was a noisy affair, eaten in a large dining hall. Lilian followed Marian as they queued up with trays and then sat down at long wooden tables. After the relative calm of the dormitory, Lilian found it all a little overwhelming. It had the feel of a medieval feast, only with awful food. She tugged at the neck of her new school jumper. It was coarse and ill-fitting, but she supposed she'd get used to it. Gazing around, she saw that up on the wood-panelled wall, there was a large tapestry. It showed two wolves curled around a flag of some kind, like a coat of arms. Turning her attention back to her meal, she prodded at the soggy quiche on her plate. A thin stream of something which looked like yellow water oozed out.

"Don't worry, we all live on biscuits and tea here," a voice at her shoulder said.

Lilian was surprised to see Serena Khan sit down beside her.

"I'm not sure it's cooked," Lilian said, eager to have the chance to build a bridge with this girl.

"Probably not," Serena said. "I always think, why risk your life when you can play it safe and just throw it in the bin?"

Lilian laughed.

"So, it's freezing cold and we all live on biscuits?" she asked.

"Yes. That's exactly it. Welcome to Shadowhall. We love it here."

Beside her, Marian laughed, too, and for a while Lilian just listened as Serena and Marian made rude comments about the school and each other. They had a curious relationship. They seemed to be both annoyed and delighted with each other and once again Lilian regretted her and Serena's tetchy first encounter. She waited until there was a pause in the conversation, before asking the question that had been on her mind.

"Who's the empty bed in our dorm room for?" she asked.

"We don't know yet," Serena said. "Another newbie, like you. Hopefully she won't immediately threaten to kill me over a seashell."

"I…no…I mean," Lilian stammered.

"Don't take the bait," Marian said. "Serena's sense of humour takes a little getting used to."

"Marian's just trying to say that I'm very unique and special," Serena said with a grin.

Lilian laughed. She already liked Marian. Serena was quickly growing on her, too. Despite the girl's rather intimidating confidence, she was funny. And almost friendly.

The other girl arrived later that night. By then they were in bed, allowed an hour of reading before lights out. The door opened and one of the prefects led the girl in. She gave Lilian, Serena and Marian a quick fearful glance as if weighing up whether they were about to eat her. Lilian was relieved to see her. It felt good to have someone else for whom this was all new and confusing.

"Girls, this is Angela Radford," the prefect said. "She

was late getting here and is very tired so please help her get comfortable."

With that, the prefect disappeared, seemingly glad to have handed over the responsibility for this younger girl's welfare. Angela was small, with mousey, thin brown hair down to her shoulders and a pinched, pale face, with a small nose and mouth. She wore large blue spectacles and peered at them like a frightened mouse.

"Hello, where are you from, Angela?" Lilian asked, trying to make the girl feel welcome. It was, after all, only a few hours ago that she'd been in the exact same position.

"Ipswich," Angela whispered.

Lilian waited to see if she would add any further detail but that was that.

"I'm Lilian," she said. "I'm new, too."

"Hi, I'm Marian," Marian said, giving her customary warm smile. "But you can call me Maz."

Serena glanced up from her book and waved her hand in a bored fashion.

"Hi, I'm Serena. You can call me...Serena."

Lilian and Marian showed Angela where she could unpack, along with directions to the bathrooms. They offered biscuits, explained about the chilly temperatures, and did their best to help Angela relax and not feel as terrified as she looked. Despite their best efforts, it didn't seem to work. Lilian could even see that Angela was trembling. She wanted to tell her it would be alright and that she was nervous, too. That Serena's bark was worse than her bite. That, yes, the school was old and a little creepy, but they would be just fine, all tucked up together. But none of that seemed appropriate with a girl she'd only just met, in a place she barely knew. And so with a tinge of regret, she left Angela to it.

It wasn't long before their door opened and Ms Strange peered in, her eyes sweeping the room like prison searchlights.

"Angela, Lilian, are you both settling in okay?" she asked. "I hope Serena and Marian are making you feel welcome?"

"Fine, thank you, miss," Lilian said.

Angela gave a tiny nod and mumbled something Lilian didn't quite catch.

"Very good. Well, it's worth remembering that while it all may seem very overwhelming right now, you'll soon get the hang of it. Goodnight then, girls. Lights out."

"Goodnight, miss," they all replied.

Lilian laid her book to one side, clicked off her bedside lamp, and settled down in bed. It felt like she was lying on a plank and she had to tightly wrap the sheets and blankets around herself before she felt even vaguely warm. Shadowhall Academy was definitely more impressive on the outside than on the inside, but she didn't mind so much. It seemed to match its personality, like some crooked, grumpy old man. Every few minutes she heard a soft sniffle come from Angela's bed. Outside, the wind rustled through the trees. A cold slap of running footsteps echoed outside in the corridor. Maybe someone coming back from one of the bathrooms. But otherwise it was silent. All things considered, her first day hadn't been bad at all. She liked her room-mates and while it felt very strange to know that her parents and sister were far away, sleeping in this shared room had begun to feel like the start of the adventure she'd always promised herself.

Lilian closed her eyes. Her mind whirled, but it wasn't long before she fell asleep. After what only seemed like a few minutes, but was probably a few hours, Lilian was awoken by the sound of murmurs and whimpers. They were coming from Angela's bed. Perhaps she was having trouble sleeping. It did feel odd to be in these unfamiliar, hard beds, with their stiff sheets that smelled of washing powder and felt like they'd been spun from iron.

Cautiously, she leaned up on one elbow and peered

across the room. It was very dark, the heavy curtains blocking out what little light there was. As her eyes adjusted, she could make out a huddled shape underneath the blankets. Angela seemed to be lying very still. Lilian waited another few seconds, before easing herself out of the sheets.

"Angela," she whispered. "Are you okay?"

In response there came a soft sniffle.

"Yes."

Lilian waited a minute, unsure what to do. There was no movement from either Marian or Serena, though she could hear their soft breathing.

"Are you sure?" Lilian said. "Did you have a nightmare or something?"

"No, I just can't sleep," Angela said.

"What is it?"

"Sshh," Angela said, holding a finger to her lips.

Lilian strained to listen. For a moment there was silence.

Then she heard it.

A faint *tap-tap-tap*.

Coming from the wall.

Chapter 3

A moment later, the tapping stopped. Angela peered at Lilian, her eyes wide and white in the gloom of the dormitory.

"It's been going on all night," Angela whispered.

"Probably just the pipes, or maybe a mouse or something," Lilian said. "You know what it's like in these old buildings."

Angela didn't look convinced.

They waited for a few more minutes, but there were no more taps. Lilian placed her hand against the wall.

"Is anybody there?" she said, in a deep, theatrical voice, hoping she could make Angela laugh.

She saw the beginning of a smile crinkle Angela's mouth, before a moment later they heard:

Tap.

On the wall.

Someone had replied.

Lilian drew back her hand in shock. Both girls stared at the wall in horror.

"Do you think someone is playing a joke on us?" Lilian said.

Angela shook her head. "If they are, it's not very funny."

"No," Lilian said. She waited another moment before placing her face close to the wall and tentatively whispering. "Hello?"

She turned and pressed her ear to it. She could hear a faint whirring noise, perhaps the heating or something, but there were no more tapping sounds.

"They've gone, I think," Lilian whispered.

Angela's eyes looked like dinner plates in the darkened dormitory. Despite herself, Lilian was pretty spooked, too.

"Come on, grab your blankets," Lilian said. "You can come and sleep with me."

"It's okay, I'm not scared," said a scared-looking Angela.

"Well, I am," Lilian said. "Come on, I need the company."

Smiling gratefully, Angela gathered up her bedclothes and together they made a comfy nest on Lilian's bed. It reminded Lilian of the times she and Susan would snuggle up together back at home.

Though as she tried to relax, Lilian found her eyes straying back to the wall.

Shadowhall Academy was proving to be unsettling in more ways than one.

The next morning, while Angela was in the bathroom brushing her teeth, Lilian told Marian and Serena what had happened.

"Medieval plumbing," Serena said, dismissively. "The last person who looked at it was probably wearing a leather jerkin and carrying a sword."

"But it seemed to answer us back," Lilian said.

"A coincidence," Serena replied. "It's an odd place at night, there are a lot of weird noises. Maybe a leaky pipe, that can sound like knocking sometimes."

"Oh," Lilian said, with a sense of relief.

As if that was the end of the matter, Serena wrapped herself in her expensive-looking dressing gown, stuck her toothbrush in her cheek and left them alone.

Lilian noticed that Marian looked troubled. She hadn't said anything when Lilian had told her about the tapping.

"What do you think?" Lilian asked her.

"It's a bit weird," she said. "Normally I wake up if I hear a pin drop. But you know there could be another explana…"

Marian trailed off as Angela entered, placing her washbag back by the bed.

"You alright, Angela?" Marian asked, breezily. "Lilian said you both had a restless night?"

Lilian noticed how quickly Marian was able to switch into normal conversation. It was slightly unnerving.

"I'm fine now," Angela said, though she looked unconvinced.

"What exactly did you hear?" Marian pressed.

"A tapping noise, right by my head. Like there was someone in the wall trying to get my attention. Lilian heard it, too. It was creepy."

"Yeah, I can imagine."

Angela turned her back on them. It appeared she didn't want to talk about it any longer. Lilian could understand that. It was hard enough talking about fears without having to do it with people you didn't know. Besides, Serena was probably right, just a normal night-time noise. There was more important stuff to consider right now.

This was the first full day of a new term in a new school and Lilian wasn't given any time to ease herself into the routine. After a breakfast of rubbery scrambled eggs, they were straight into lessons. Lilian tried her best to focus, though it was hard when everything and everyone was new. She made a point of not answering any questions in class, even though she knew a lot of the answers. She didn't want to draw attention to herself on day one.

Walking between the lessons gave Lilian a chance to get to know the layout of the school. Even on a sunny day like this, the light never seemed to penetrate inside. The hallways remained gloomy and cold. The classrooms were dark, the wood panels seeming to slurp up any sunlight that dare creep inside. And apart from the bustling dining hall, there was a hush about the place despite the number of people in it. Lilian thought it a slightly peculiar atmosphere, more akin to a church or a museum than a busy school.

Later, she had a history class with Mr Bullen, who seemed as nervous and distracted in the classroom as he was out of it, his eyes always darting around, his hands clenching and unclenching, as if he had other more important and terrible business on his mind than teaching children. Yet although the classes moved fast, and there was a lot of information to take in, and she was surrounded by lots of obviously smart girls, Lilian didn't feel too out of her depth.

From time to time she caught the eye of her roommates. Marian always returned her smile. Serena rolled her eyes as if this was one of the worst ordeals of her life. Angela always looked away, a fierce blaze on her cheeks. Lilian hoped things would improve for her. Happily, her own first-day nerves were rapidly disappearing. She'd even begun to get the geography of the place, confident that she could now find her way to both the dining hall and their dormitory.

Later, after another disappointing dinner, the four girls sat on their beds. Angela hadn't spoken much and so Lilian tried again.

"How was your first day, Angela?" she asked.

Angela glanced up from her book with that rabbit-in-the-headlights look.

"It was okay."

"It's confusing here, isn't it?" Lilian said, coming to sit on the end of Angela's bed.

"Yes."

"What's Ipswich like then?"

"It's okay."

"Um…what do your parents do?"

"My dad works for the government. He has a new job that makes him travel abroad a lot, that's why he sent me here."

"And your mum?"

"She died when I was five."

"I'm sorry."

"It's okay, I don't really remember her."

They lapsed into silence. Lilian got the distinct impression that Angela didn't want to talk.

"Well, if you…you know…get scared in the night or anything, you can wake me up, I won't mind. We can always make a camp on my bed again."

Angela's pale eyes flickered for a moment, as if a memory had just drifted across her mind.

"Thanks."

Lilian returned to her own bed. Marian looked up and raised her eyebrows.

"Any luck?" she whispered.

Lilian just shook her head. At least she'd tried.

*   *   *

Later, just before lights out, Lilian went to the bathroom to brush her teeth. About to go in, she paused. She could hear somebody talking. It sounded like Angela was having a conversation, though Lilian could only hear Angela's voice.

"…who's there…? I can hear you, you know…"

Lilian opened the door. Angela was at the last sink down, peering into the mirror. She jumped a little as the door opened and turned to look at Lilian.

"Sorry if I startled you," Lilian said.

Angela glanced back into the mirror but didn't reply.

Behind Lilian, the door blew open a fraction. Shivering, she turned and closed it, before standing at the sink next to Angela.

"Who were you talking to?" Lilian said, squeezing out some toothpaste.

"I thought I heard whispering behind the wall," Angela said, splashing some water on her face with a slight shudder.

Lilian strained to listen, but she couldn't hear anything.

"I think it's just me and you," she said.

"Yes, sorry, I don't know what it was. You probably think I'm weird, talking to myself."

"No, not at all. I do the same thing sometimes."

"Talk to yourself?"

"Yes. I like intelligent conversation."

Angela laughed then, her whole demeanour brightening, as if she'd just felt the sun on her face.

"You know it'll get better, don't you?" Lilian said, spitting out a mouthful of toothpaste.

"I just find it hard to talk to people I don't know. I get shy and my words get jumbled up and that makes me even more nervous."

Lilian felt like she'd just spoken to the real Angela for the first time.

"We're all shy and nervous inside," Lilian said. "Some people just hide it better."

"And I think our dormitory is haunted."

Lilian paused, wondering if Angela was joking, but she appeared deadly earnest.

"Yes, I think it is, too," she said eventually. "It's haunted by four girls with tired eyes who live on nothing but biscuits."

Angela gave her a faint smile. But what she'd said made Lilian think. Not just the dormitory, but the school itself had an unnerving atmosphere to it. Was it just because it was old? Or was there more here than met the eye?

They returned to the dormitory together. Marian and

Serena were already in bed. Even though it was only September, the nights were growing longer, and their dormitory was one of those rooms that seemed to suck the cold air into every nook and cranny and crevice, before slowly blowing it back over them.

"What have you two been doing?" Serena said. "Hatching escape plans?"

"We were just saying what amazing room-mates we have," Lilian said. "And how lucky we feel."

Marian burst out laughing. Serena grinned.

"Yes, you're both very fortunate to be sharing a room with me and Spooky here."

"I don't know about that," Marian said. "I'd say you both drew the short straw."

After lights out, despite what Angela had said about strange whispers in the bathroom, Lilian went to sleep with a smile on her face. Angela was going to be okay. *She* was going to be okay. And joking aside, she really did feel as if she'd got lucky with her room-mates. Marian and Serena were both very different – but very cool.

Thankfully, that night was untroubled, and Lilian didn't hear Angela make a sound.

Though she did notice that their dormitory door was slightly ajar when she woke.

She was positive it had been shut when they went to bed.

"Did Angela hear any more creepy tapping last night?" Serena asked.

Lilian, Serena and Marian were in the library for study hour, time they could use to catch up on homework, read, or if you were Serena, whisper very loudly about things that had made you curious.

"No, I don't think so," Lilian said. "Where is she anyway?"

"I think she's with Mrs Benson, the nurse," Marian said, twizzling the spiky ends of her hair between her fingers. "She told me she wasn't feeling too well."

"Really?" Lilian said. "I hope it's nothing serious."

"Probably her nerves," Serena said. "She comes across as a frightened little kitten."

"I'd be frightened about sharing a bedroom with you, too," Marian said, which earned her a chuckle from Lilian and a flick on the hair from Serena.

"Girls," Miss Coates, the librarian called. "You know, the art of conversation is a truly wonderful gift and you're all so brilliant at it – just not right now, okay?"

Chastened, they picked up their books and pretended to be engrossed. But there was something nagging at the back of Lilian's mind. Something Marian had said. Or something Marian had *nearly* said when Lilian had told her about the tapping on the wall.

"Marian," Lilian whispered as quiet as she could, while keeping one eye on Miss Coates. "What were you going to say yesterday, about the noise in the wall? You know, before Angela came back from the bathroom?"

Marian gave her own furtive glance towards the librarian.

"Well, I didn't want to say anything in front of Angela. But did you know that Shadowhall is haunted?" she said.

Lilian's mouth dropped open.

"Oh, not this again," Serena said, a little too loudly.

"Come on, girls," Miss Coates called. "You have all the time in the world to chat, except this teeny-tiny little hour when we ask you to be quiet. I have every faith that you can rise to the challenge!"

They fell silent then. Lilian peered at Marian and raised her eyebrows, but Marian held a finger to her lips before pointing out of the door, as if to say she would tell her later. Lilian wasn't sure what to think about ghosts. She tended to believe there was a rational explanation for most things. Nevertheless, she was intrigued, not to mention unsettled.

And so, once their study hour was done, Lilian pulled Marian to one side in the corridor.

"So what's this about the school being haunted?" she said.

"It's true," Marian said. "There's a ghost. Lots of girls have heard her."

"Heard who?"

"Cold Mary," Marian said. "She died here."

Despite herself, Lilian felt the skin on her arms prickle.

"Died? What happened?"

Marian glanced around. They were standing to one side, while a sea of girls washed past, on their way to their last lesson before dinner.

"It happened a long time ago, I'm not sure when exactly. But on the day school broke up for October half-term, a group of girls were playing hide-and-seek upstairs, and a girl called Mary Atkins crawled through a hatch into a space behind the walls. She thought it was the perfect hiding place, nobody would find her in there – and she was right. One by one, the girls were all found, but despite looking everywhere, they couldn't find Mary. They called for her and told her she had won, but when she didn't answer they assumed she'd just given up and gone home. But Mary had squeezed into such a small space that she got stuck fast. She banged and knocked and shouted but most girls had left the school with their parents by then, and the ones who remained, along with just a few members of staff...well, they were all downstairs on the lower levels and couldn't hear her. It was bitterly cold, but because the school was going to be empty, they'd turned the heating off. Mary cried and yelled but it was no good. By the time Mary's parents realized she hadn't made her train home for the holidays and had alerted the school, it was too late. They found her there, in the wall, all blue and stiff. And now she comes back to Shadowhall, knocking on the walls, trying to tell everyone where she is."

"Ugh, that's horrible," Lilian said. She'd been transfixed as Marian spoke, imagining the terror of the girl when she realized she'd become trapped. "Why did it take so long for anyone to notice she was missing?"

"The day before any holiday is pretty hectic. People coming in and out all day. They just assumed she'd gone home with her parents."

"And so she froze to death?"

"Froze, starved, hypothermia or something, I'm not really sure. But when they found her, her skin was blue, and her fingers were frozen into crooked knots. They pulled her body out through a hatch in the dormitory wall."

"A dormitory," Lilian said, aghast. "Which one?"

Marian pursed her lips.

"Take a guess."

Chapter 4

Lilian examined Marian's expression, trying to see if she could make out the beginning of a smile, or maybe the hint of a smirk. Something that would reveal Marian was actually joking. With nothing on offer, Lilian had to come straight out and say it.

"Our dormitory? Is this a wind-up, Maz?"

Marian shook her head furiously.

"I might be a goth, but I wouldn't joke about someone dying."

Lilian wondered if this wasn't some kind of new-girl test.

"And you're not just trying to scare me?"

"No, lots of girls have heard her. That's why Ms Strange doesn't need to patrol the corridors at night.

Most girls are too frightened to leave their bedrooms once the lights go out, in case Cold Mary tries to drag them inside the walls with her. The only reason anyone goes out alone at night here is if they're so desperate to pee they just can't hold it in! Anyway, you heard her for yourself."

"I heard tapping, yes, but I'm not sure it was this… *Cold Mary*," Lilian said. Despite herself, her skin felt especially icy right now. She glanced at one of the walls, the image of a blue-skinned girl suddenly refusing to leave her mind.

"Have *you* heard her?" Lilian said.

Marian nodded slowly.

"Late at night, around the school, yes. You can't help but get a bit scared. But I just think that if I don't bother her, then she won't bother me. Anyway, I'd like to be a ghost one day."

"Well, I don't believe in ghosts," Lilian added, just to let Marian know that she wasn't scared.

"Ghosts don't care what you think, Lilian," Marian sniffed. "They believe in you. Besides, you've heard it yourself now, and if it isn't a ghost, then what is it? Walls don't tap themselves. Look, I have to go call my mum, she's been a bit poorly. I'll see you at supper – we can talk more later. You know how to find your way down there, don't you?"

Lilian nodded.

"Yes, thanks, Maz, see you down there."

Lilian watched Marian go. What she'd said had been pretty creepy – *Ghosts believe in you.* She imagined that was a very *goth* thing to say. Lilian wandered back through the corridors, unsure of what to do with the hour before supper. In the end she found herself outside her dorm. She hesitated a second before pushing open the door. Had a girl really died in here? The thought was unsettling. If it was true, and she still had her doubts despite Marian's insistence, which part of the wall had Cold Mary been found in?

Lilian shook her head. This story about Cold Mary was getting to her. And yet, though she tried to push it out of her mind, Lilian had to admit – Marian had a point.

Tapping on walls had to have an explanation.

So, if that reason wasn't a ghost, then what was it?

Lilian had an idea.

As she walked into her dorm room, she was somewhat surprised to see Angela and Serena sitting together on Serena's bed. Both had their legs crossed and were staring at each other, seemingly mid-conversation. Just like old pals. Angela even had a smile on her face.

"Hello," Lilian said. "What are you up to?"

"Well, I've just discovered that Angela can actually talk, long sentences and everything," Serena said, flashing Angela a smile. "But what are *you* up to, Lilian? You look like you've seen a ghost. Marian's been telling you all about Cold Mary, I assume?"

"Who's Cold Mary?" Angela said, sitting up on her haunches with a frown, like she'd just caught a whiff of a foul smell.

Lilian hadn't planned on relaying Marian's story to Angela. She looked scared enough of everything as it was. But Serena had landed her in it.

"Oh, okay, well you know that tapping in the wall...?" Lilian said.

Angela nodded with wide eyes.

Sighing, Lilian gave Angela a shortened account of the Cold Mary story, trying her best to sound casual and nonchalant about it all, so that Angela didn't get too freaked out. Besides, she also had her own plan to prove Marian wrong.

"That's who we heard then!" Angela cried. "It all makes sense. Oh, I'm not sure I can sleep another night in here."

"Marian sees ghosts and ghouls everywhere she looks, I wouldn't worry about it," Serena said. "Though the whole tapping thing is a bit creepy, I'll give her that."

"Well, hang on one moment," Lilian said, raising a finger. "I think it may be something else altogether. And I can prove it."

"You can?" Angela said, looking relieved.

"Yes," Lilian said. "Meet me back here after dinner."

After they'd chased a rather anaemic piece of beef around their plates, squashed a few soggy roast potatoes with their forks, and totally ignored a pile of cabbage that had been boiled to within an inch of its life, Lilian and the girls met back in the dormitory to hear what she had to say.

Serena, Marian and Angela sat on Serena's bed, waiting with expectant expressions. Lilian felt a stab of nerves. Now she had to go through with a plan that was starting to feel very stupid. Too late now though.

"What if", Lilian said, "I could prove to you that the tapping in the wall isn't Cold Mary?"

"I would be very happy because then I get to laugh at Marian for making up stories," Serena said, aiming a sly grin in Marian's direction.

"Personally, I would be very surprised," Marian said. "It's not my story, I'm just relaying what I've been told. And what I've heard in the walls on dark, winter nights," she added, ominously.

"I would be very relieved," Angela added, with a nervous giggle.

Lilian pointed above Angela's bed.

"Can you see that square in the middle of the wall? It's painted over but I think it's an old hatch. Earlier, I looked at all the walls in this entire room and this is the only opening I can see."

"It's not...*the* hatch, is it?" Angela said, with a noticeable flicker of unease. "You know, the one from the story."

"No, I don't believe it is," Lilian replied, confidently. "And if we stand on your bed, we can get it open and see what's inside. And I bet we'll find something loose. Or a mouse nest. Or a leaky pipe, like Serena said. Mystery solved. I just need a chisel or something to get it open."

"Will an old nail file do?" Marian said.

"Perfect," Lilian said.

A few minutes later, she was standing on Angela's bed, nail file in hand, frowning at the wall.

"Hmm, I'll have to do a bit of scraping, get this paint

off. Angela, fetch a sheet from my bed and we'll put it on yours, then it won't get covered in paint chips and we can make it all neat and tidy afterwards."

They laid the sheet on the bed, then Lilian leaned up and scraped around the edges of the hatch until she'd cleared it of paint. It made more of a mess than she intended, and now the wall was scuffed and marked.

"I think I might have made a mistake," she said.

"We can't stop now!" Serena cried. "Besides, don't worry, Jesus can give us a hand." She pointed to the picture on the wall. "We can hang him over the hatch once we're done. Nobody will ever notice."

It was a good idea. Relieved, Lilian pushed the nail file into the side of the hatch and prised at it with all her strength. There was a cracking, splintering sound, followed by a mini waterfall of paint flecks, before the hatch popped open and Lilian found herself staring into a very dark space.

"Don't suppose you've got a torch, too, Maz?" Lilian said.

"Give me one sec," Marian said.

Moments later, Lilian shone Marian's torch into the hole she'd made. Dust motes floated through the beam of light. Thick spiderwebs gathered in between the beams and there was a rank smell of what Lilian thought was probably mouse droppings, which in one way was good, because it backed up her theory. But she was on tiptoes and couldn't see very far in.

"Can someone give me a leg-up?" she said.

"Is this how the *Cold Lilian* story starts?" Serena said.

"Please be careful, Lilian," Angela said, solemnly.

Lilian didn't know whose hands gripped the soles of her feet and pushed, but with the added momentum she was able to pull herself further into the gap. She rested her chest on a wooden beam, which allowed her to move her arms, as if she was swimming. Looking around, it felt like she'd opened a time capsule. The beams appeared ancient, built as they were from gnarled oak that was so old it looked almost black, each one studded with huge great nails. They criss-crossed the space within, creating what resembled a very sturdy climbing frame. But the gaps in between the beams were narrow. Someone small could quite easily get in here, behind the walls – perhaps even climb up through and around the beams. Yet there were places where you could get stuck if you weren't careful. The thought made her shiver.

She looked around for mouse nests but couldn't see any signs of life. Shining the torch up revealed pipes that looked more modern. A later addition perhaps. But there were no drips coming from them or pools of water on the floor that might indicate a leak. A cold breath fanned across her face. If she thought it was chilly in the bedroom, it was like an oasis compared to in here. It was cold enough to freeze.

"How's the investigation going?" Marian called. "Any skeletons turned up yet?"

"No," said Lilian, her voice muffled against the neck of her sweater.

As she shone the torch around one more time, something glinted down below on one of the beams. It appeared to be something metallic. Lilian strained to reach it but couldn't get close.

"Can someone hold my feet?" she asked. "I've found something."

"Maybe you should come down now?" Angela said, sounding panicked.

"I just have to get this thing I've seen; someone grab my ankles."

A moment later, Lilian felt Serena tighten her hands around Lilian's legs.

"Okay, I've got you."

"I'm just going to lean down," Lilian said. "Don't let go."

Twisting her body between the beams, she turned so that her right arm could stretch out. Her fingers touched wood. Suddenly, she lurched forwards and she felt Serena's hand tighten around her ankles.

"Oops, sorry about that," Serena said. "I've got you now."

Breathing deeply, Lilian inched her fingertips over the rough surface, until she felt them close upon something cold and metallic. She heard a soft rattle as she gathered it into her palm.

"Okay, got it, pull me back," she panted.

She heard Serena grunt and, thankfully, felt herself move back up. Gripping the beam, she pushed herself along it. She looked down at her palm. She'd found a necklace or bracelet of some kind. If it had got stuck there, maybe that could have been tapping against something?

But then she had another, more chilling thought – maybe it had belonged to Cold Mary? If so, it was ironic that her mission to disprove the story about the trapped girl had only confirmed it to be true – but she would have to take a closer look at it. Right now, she wanted to get out of this cramped, cold space. Inching her legs back, she shuffled towards the hatch opening. About to pull herself out, she heard a quiet thump.

Swinging the torch up, she caught movement. A figure, darting between the wooden beams, as if trying to escape the light from Lilian's torch. Lilian swung the torch around the space again, shining it into every nook and cranny where someone might be hiding, but it soon became clear that there was nobody in there except her.

Heart thudding against her ribs, she quickly pushed herself back out and landed feet first on Angela's bed.

"Okay?" Marian asked.

Lilian didn't have time to answer.

The door to their dorm room swung open and Ms Strange the headmistress looked at them with wide, horrified eyes.

"Oh, I'm sorry," she said, her voice grating like gravel. "Forgive my intrusion. I didn't realize you were busy destroying the school's walls."

"It's not what it looks like," Marian said lamely, her hair drooping into her eyes as if it knew how she was feeling.

"No?" Ms Strange said. "Well, my eyes must be deceiving me because it looks like there's a gaping big hole in the wall and paint all over the bed and the floor."

Nobody said anything.

"Very well, if there's nothing more to it, then you'll all

report to my office tomorrow. Serena, Marian, I expect you to set a better example. Lilian, Angela, let's just say you haven't exactly made a fantastic first impression. Now, please get this mess cleaned up and go to bed. Come to my office at lunchtime and we can discuss this further."

Lilian had been standing on Angela's bed. As Ms Strange shut the door, she sat down and placed her head in her hands. Someone touched her on the shoulder.

"Don't worry, Lilian," Serena said. "Ms Strange isn't as fierce as she seems. It'll all be forgotten in a few days."

But Lilian wasn't thinking about being in trouble. That would come later. What she couldn't get out of her mind was what she'd seen, just before she'd slid back out of the wall.

The darting figure of a young girl.

Chapter 5

Lilian didn't dare mention what she'd seen to her dorm mates. Not to Marian, who would undoubtedly be delighted at news of Lilian's creepy sighting. Nor to Serena, who would probably try and laugh it off or explain it away. Certainly not to Angela, who had to sleep beneath the hatch and was already jumping at shadows.

After Ms Strange had left they'd managed to get the hatch closed, and using a sheet to catch the dried paint had meant they'd been able to tidy everything up. As Lilian pressed her head into the pillow, she wondered if she'd been mistaken about what she'd seen. Torches, shadows, dust, thick wooden beams, frayed nerves, perhaps they all combined in her mind, creating something that wasn't really there? At least, that's what Lilian desperately tried to tell herself. The only problem was the other Lilian. The one who had actually been there and witnessed it for herself. That Lilian could recall seeing what had appeared to be a young girl, caught in the torchlight for the briefest moment, as if trapped like a fly in amber. That Lilian also remembered the sheer terror she'd felt. It was only now, an hour or two later, that her heartbeat had returned to normal.

So, what to do?

She'd briefly looked at the object she'd found. It was a necklace. The other girls had all tried to have a closer look as well, but it was too dark after lights out and none of them wanted to switch the torch back on in case Ms Strange was still lurking outside. Now it was tucked away in Lilian's bedroom drawer.

Lilian knew she had to find out more about Cold Mary. There had been no evidence of anything else that might cause a tapping in the wall. Mice certainly couldn't make a noise that loud. And the only thing she'd seen, apart from the necklace, had looked like a young girl. But as there weren't any real, alive girls running around behind the walls – what had she seen? A ghost? Cold Mary herself?

Lilian shivered. She wasn't going to be looking in there

again anytime soon. Also, she was already in trouble and she'd barely even started the term. She hadn't ever been in trouble at school before. What was she thinking? Lilian rolled onto her side and pulled her knees up to her chest, her quiet groan of anguish sounding a little ghostly in the darkness of the dormitory.

There had been no more tapping noises that night. The next morning at breakfast, Lilian pushed a spoon through her lumpy porridge and sighed. She was already finding it hard to be enthusiastic about the food at Shadowhall, but now – served with a heavy pinch of dread about what she saw last night and what would happen when they saw Ms Strange – she simply couldn't stomach it. Knowing she needed to keep her energy up, she managed to make do with a banana and a glass of apple juice.

"I'm sorry I got you all in trouble," she said to her dorm mates, who sat opposite her pushing their spoons through their porridge.

"It's fine," Serena said. "You know, we could have said, 'No, Lilian, we don't want to look inside the wall.' We make our own decisions."

"That's right," Marian said. "And where one goes...

I mean, where goes one, all go... Oh well, you know what I mean."

"At least we didn't find any bones," Angela said, with a shrug.

Lilian stayed silent. There might not have been any bones, but she'd seen something...someone...that had no right being there. She wondered whether now was a good time to mention it and decided not. One hurdle at a time.

"Did you get a chance to take a closer look at that necklace yet?" asked Serena, interrupting her thoughts.

Lilian pulled it out of her pocket, and the others all leaned forward, each taking turns to hold it in their hand. It was a curious piece. A necklace, the silver tarnished with age. It looked very old. Like an antique. Lilian even wondered if it might be worth something. But more perplexing was the thing attached to the necklace. It was a silver charm, which Serena popped open with her fingernail.

"There's an initial inside," Serena said. "Look!"

They all craned their necks forward.

It was a C.

"That's pretty nice," Marian said. "I wonder who C is?"

"Maybe it means 'Cold'?" Angela said. "You know, Cold Mary?"

"I doubt she had time to get a necklace made while she was trapped in the wall," Serena said.

It was meant as a joke, but none of them laughed. It didn't really seem like a laughing matter. Once again, the image of the girl running through the torchlight appeared in Lilian's head, but try as she might, she couldn't be entirely sure that it wasn't a mistake. It had only been a brief flash. A split-second sighting. Which made her wonder, was it all just a combination of a trick of the light and Marian's ghost story?

"It is mysterious though," Lilian said, softly. "And it might be really old. We should probably give it to Ms Strange when we go up and see her."

"We'll never see it again if that happens," Marian said. "Finders keepers!"

"We could at least keep it until we find out more about it?" Angela suggested.

It was a good idea and Lilian didn't really want to surrender it before she'd had time to study it further. Who *was* C? Was it perhaps someone Cold Mary had known? If it wasn't anything to do with her, then why was it lost behind the wall of their dormitory? Did it have anything to do with the tapping?

Thinking about its age gave Lilian an idea. She could ask

Mr Bullen – history was his speciality after all. She made a note to go and see him about it. If he said it was valuable, then she could hand it over to him for safekeeping. Lilian placed it back in her pocket. It was time for lessons and then the dreaded meeting with Ms Strange.

As she sat in class, learning about the six wives of Henry VIII, followed by the causes of coastal erosion, followed by how to ask where the train station was in French, Lilian found it hard to concentrate. All last night's events swirled around her head, and she couldn't shake the hollow feeling in her stomach when she thought about how she'd got both herself and her new dorm mates in trouble. It was the kind of first school experience that she wouldn't be telling her parents about and she hoped Ms Strange wouldn't tell them either.

As the lunch bell rang, the girls trudged up the stairs to Ms Strange's office; she made them wait for ten minutes before calling them in with a steely glare.

Before Ms Strange had a chance to speak, Lilian gave a full confession that she'd rehearsed earlier. She told Ms Strange that Angela hadn't been able to sleep because of a knocking in the wall, and rather than bother anyone, Lilian thought she might be able to get to the bottom of the problem herself. She didn't think it would turn out to be as messy as it was and she was sorry and had since cleaned it all up. It was a version of the truth. She just hadn't mentioned Cold Mary, that's all.

Ms Strange listened to all of this with pursed lips and an unimpressed expression.

"I see," she said. "Well, thank you for explaining, Lilian. I'll concede that I initially thought this an act of wanton vandalism, so this helps clear things up. However, I still don't like the fact that the wall will need repainting and you insisted on doing all this without bothering to mention the problem to a teacher first. You may think we're here just for the fun of it, but we're actually here to help and if you have any issues whatsoever, we should always be the first port of call."

"Yes, Ms Strange, sorry," Lilian said.

"Yet you were trying to help your new dormitory friend," Ms Strange said, getting to her feet and opening her office door. "And so, if you girls give me a hand right now, then we'll forget all about it."

The girls looked at each other with bewildered expressions. It sounded like a trap. But they dutifully followed Ms Strange along the corridor, towards the back of the school. Two girls in their year, Sarah Shoesmith and Sally Baldwin, smirked at them as they passed.

Ha ha, you're in trouble.

Serena flashed them a scowl which seemed to do the trick.

Ms Strange led them downstairs, then descended again to the basement.

Lilian hadn't been down here yet.

The lights were dimmer, more of a dull yellow than the bright whites of the dining hall. The floor was like a tumbledown road, cracked and split and uneven. It smelled musty, as though the air had been breathed in and out many times before. There was a dripping noise coming from somewhere. A red fire extinguisher had been made grey with dust and cobwebs.

Marian nudged Lilian in the shoulder and pointed to a wood-panelled door, on which a small handwritten note had been stuck.

Simon Bullen, History & Antiquities.

Please knock before entering.

Marian whispered in Lilian's ear.

"Notice it's down in the basement where there's no sunlight."

Lilian stifled a giggle. Now was not the time to be laughing. Not if she wanted to repair her reputation with Ms Strange.

Ms Strange led them past Mr Bullen's office, towards another door. Fishing out a key, she unlocked it and gestured inside. It was small, cramped and full of cardboard boxes. Empty shelves lined the walls, most of the boxes having been dumped in a pile in the middle of the room, the contents spilling onto the floor.

"The caretaker had a little accident while they were moving this in here," Ms Strange said. "But they were called away to another more urgent job and haven't had a chance to clear it up yet so I thought we could help. You see, there's a lot of important school history contained in these boxes. Nothing compared to Mr Bullen's artefacts of course, but still very interesting. So, girls, if you could get the contents packed away neatly and onto the shelves, then like I say, we'll call it quits and forget all about the damaged paintwork on the wall of your dormitory. Try and keep everything in order where possible. I shall be back in an hour; please have it done by then."

Then, with a final frown, Ms Strange gusted away.

The girls gazed around the room. It was hard to know where to start. Just piles of boxes and what looked like photographs and sheafs of paper forming a giant heap.

"What a mess," Serena said.

"What did Ms Strange mean about *Mr Bullen's*

artefacts?" Lilian asked. It sounded very intriguing.

"She means his victims," Marian said, wiggling her fingers together as if they were claws. "They're all hung upside down in his office where he drains them of blood, but of course that would put the parents off from sending their children here, so she calls them *his artefacts.*"

This time Lilian did laugh, though she noted the confusion on Angela's face.

"Marian has a theory that Mr Bullen is a vampire, that's all it is," Lilian explained. "But seriously, what did she mean?"

"Well, you know this place used to be a private home?" Serena said. "There's stuff left over – you know, furniture, art and stuff. He's in charge of it because he's the history teacher. There's another storeroom next to his office."

"I'd love to see that sometime," Lilian said. "I like seeing old things. I always try and imagine the people who owned them."

"I'm sure he'd love to show you," Marian said, before putting on a creepy voice. "But that would be the last thing anyone ever saw of you…ha…ha…ha."

"Okay, cut the vampire chat, Spooky," Serena said. "Let's get this done and we can get out of this hole."

They started at the top of the pile, placing the contents

back into the boxes before tying string around each lid and putting them back on the shelves. With four of them working it didn't take long before the pile began to shrink. Lilian gave the contents of the boxes a quick glance every now and then, just out of curiosity. There were photographs of old school sports days, everyone running around in the navy and gold athletic outfits of Shadowhall Academy. Photos of musicals and school plays, too, the girls dressed up with too much stage make-up and comically exaggerated expressions.

The last two boxes Lilian set about organizing contained framed classroom photographs. Maybe they had once hung on a wall somewhere. While the others huffed and puffed around her, Lilian took a closer look. In some way it felt like she was looking at an earlier version of herself. Here were hundreds of girls, just like her, frozen in time as they stared at the camera. And now here she was, walking the same halls and corridors.

The framed photos were all dated, and as she sorted her way through them from top to bottom, the older they got. It was like going back in time. Lilian could see hairstyles change. The style of glasses that the teachers and pupils wore. The cut of the uniforms. The quality of the photography, too, from modern 1980s photos, to the more faded shots of the seventies and sixties, right back to fuzzy black and white photos, which began around the 1940s. Feeling drawn into the history of the school, Lilian leafed through them, wondering what had happened to all these girls and their teachers. Where did they go? What did they do with their lives? It was both fascinating and a little disorientating. So many girls, all like her, each with their own thoughts and ideas and ambitions.

Along the bottom of the photographs were the names of the girls, ordered from left to right, so you could look at the name and then match it to the relevant girl in the photograph. Lilian had nearly reached the end of the pile when she paused, seeing a name she recognized.

Marilyn Strange.

Lilian peered at the photograph. A young girl with shoulder-length dark hair scowled back at her.

"Hey, look at this," she said. "You'll never guess who went to school here."

Intrigued, the girls gathered around. Serena let out a bark of laughter.

"Well, I never! Ms Strange used to be one of us!"

"Hello, who's this, too?" Marian said, stabbing her finger against a name.

Theresa Coates.

"Who's that?" Angela asked.

Marian pointed to the grinning blonde-haired young girl in the photograph.

"That's Miss Coates, the librarian. She takes us for study hour. She's really nice."

"That's two of them got sucked back into Shadowhall," Serena said. "Hope that doesn't happen to us! Imagine never being able to escape this place."

Lilian's laughter caught in her throat. Here was another name she recognized. Pulling the photograph closer to her face, she stared at a name that made her skin grow cold.

Mary Atkins.

Or, as she came to be known…

Cold Mary.

Chapter 6

Lilian traced the name on the photograph, but to her disappointment, it appeared that Mary Atkins was partially hidden behind another girl. Lilian stared at the photograph, willing Mary to reveal herself. But it was a moment frozen in time and Mary would forever be concealed behind a grinning girl with pigtails. There was just the hint of a dark eye, the curve of a nose, a mouth that could have been smiling, it was hard to tell. In one way, it seemed a suitable photograph of someone who was now a ghost. She was there and she wasn't. Hidden from view for evermore.

But she *was* real.

That was the important thing. And Lilian didn't quite know what to make of it. She'd been convinced that the

Cold Mary story was just a story, an exaggeration, a tall tale designed to scare new girls. But now what? She'd heard the knocking. She'd seen what looked like a young girl behind the wall. Could it be true? Was Shadowhall Academy haunted?

She was reminded of something her dad had said once. Lilian, Susan and their parents had got into a discussion about ghosts. His exact words had stuck in her head for some reason.

I'm not sure about ghosts, but I do believe that bad or sad events can sometimes leave an imprint on a place.

What her dad had meant, as Lilian understood it, was that places could remember bad or tragic events, just like people could. It explained why some people would get a weird feeling about somewhere they visited. They might suddenly find themselves feeling sad, or anxious, or scared. They might hear footsteps in an empty house. Scratching in the night. Faint whispers of conversation that had no obvious source. It could apply to smells, too. People might get a waft of perfume, or tobacco, as if an invisible spirit had just walked by. So maybe, because of what happened to Mary, there was still an echo of her inside the school?

The other girls sensed Lilian's shock.

"What is it?" Marian said. "Why is your mouth hanging open?"

All Lilian could do was point to the name.

"Told you she was real," Marian said, quietly.

"How sad," Angela added. "I wonder how long after this photo was taken that she...well, you know."

"We'll never hear the end of this now," Serena said. "Marian will be whispering about it in our ears every night when we're trying to get to sleep."

"So, there is a real ghost then?" Angela said, her eyes wide behind her glasses.

"Maybe?" Lilian said, feeling a chill descend on her. "But there's no need for you to be afraid, Angela. Ghosts can't hurt you."

"Can't they?" Marian said. "Are you sure about that, Lilian?"

"Oh, what are we going to do?" Angela said, her voice trembling.

"We're going to stick together and look after one another," Lilian said. She looked at each of them in turn. "Okay?"

"We stick together," Serena said, grimly.

"Agreed," Marian said. "Safety in numbers, okay, Angela?"

Angela nodded, though she didn't look too reassured.

In the meantime, if Lilian wanted to find out more about Mary Atkins and whether she truly was a restless spirit, then she needed the full facts about what had happened back then. There was no way she would bring the subject up with Ms Strange, not being in her good books right now. But Miss Coates seemed nice and approachable and she'd been in Mary's class too. She had to know something. Lilian resolved to get up to the library at the earliest opportunity.

Ms Strange arrived a few minutes later and cast her eyes around the storeroom.

"Good job, girls," she said. "Now get yourselves off to lessons."

The rest of the day passed in a blur of sums, dates, scientific formulas and medieval poems, so it wasn't until lunchtime the next day that Lilian was able to get away to the library. Thankfully, the night before had been quiet. No sounds from the walls, which meant Angela was safe to sleep in her own bed. Lilian had also remembered about the necklace she found and placed it in her school bag to ask Mr Bullen about later. But first, Miss Coates.

Lilian told the girls what she had planned and rushed her lunch so she would have plenty of time to get to the library before her first lesson in the afternoon. With most of the school sat in the canteen staring despondently at their plates, the corridors were quiet. The library was up on the second floor. Reaching it, she pushed the door open. It appeared to be empty. Apparently, this room had also served as the original library back when Shadowhall Academy used to be a private home. The school had modernized it, but it retained enough of the original character for Lilian to be able to imagine it back as it might once have been. Comfortable chairs that wrapped you up like a thick blanket. The tall windows looking out over the blustery gardens and to the treeline beyond. The dark, seasoned wood of the shelves, making the air smell aged and preserved, soaking up any bright light so that it always felt pleasantly gloomy. The dust motes that rose from the musty paper like a living, ever-moving galaxy of stars. Lilian walked down towards the back of the library and immediately saw Miss Coates, sitting at her desk, nose buried in a book while balancing a sandwich in her hand.

Lilian already liked Miss Coates. In a place where many things were rigid and dull, Miss Coates appeared to buck the rules. Her clothes were always colourful and bright, which stood out against the school uniforms and the grey suits that most of the other teachers seemed to prefer. Her hair sprang out in all directions, as if it was deliriously happy. She wore purple eyeshadow and red lipstick. Her earrings were shaped like jade arrowheads. Bracelets and bangles rattled on both her wrists. Blue framed glasses hung on a golden chain around her neck. If Mr Bullen was a dark whisper, then Miss Coates was a joyous shout.

She looked up when she heard Lilian approach and smiled.

"Hello, Lilian. Come to do some extra study? Can I help you find anything?"

Lilian wondered how best to broach the subject of Mary Atkins and whether Miss Coates knew anything about how she died. She couldn't just come out and say it.

"Um…hi…I was just looking for something to read in bed tonight."

Miss Coates folded a bookmark into her book and placed it on her desk.

"Well, guess who came to the right place? Reading while horizontal and covered in blankets is one of my favourite things to do, too. Anything particular in mind?"

"Hmm." Lilian twisted her palms together and did her best to look casual. "Do you have any books about... ghosts?"

"Ghosts?" Miss Coates said, the smile dropping off her face. "As in ghost stories? Are you sure that's the best subject matter for late-night reading?"

"No, I mean, more about the science of ghosts, and you know, the paranormal."

Miss Coates got to her feet. "Well, that's a request I've not had before. How curious. I seem to remember we have some that may fit the bill. Let's go and look, shall we?"

She led Lilian up and down a few rows, pausing every now and then to frown at a book spine or two. Finally, she pulled one out and showed Lilian the title.

Ghosts: The Evidence Examined.

"This one seems to match the brief, Lilian. What do you think?"

"Perfect," Lilian replied. "This should help a lot."

As they made their way back to Miss Coates's desk so she could put a stamp in the book with its return date, Miss Coates asked the question that Lilian hoped she might.

"Do you mind me asking why you're interested in ghosts?"

Lilian took a deep breath. It was now or never.

"Marian, my room-mate, she told us that there's a ghost in this school called Cold Mary. But I'm not sure I believe her. I wanted to see what the experts say."

Miss Coates's face sagged a little and, for a moment, she stared off into space, as if a memory had just waved hello.

"Oh, so *that* story is doing the rounds again, is it?"

"You've heard it before?" Lilian pressed. "Is it all just made up then?"

"Much of it is, yes," Miss Coates said. "But there's a truth to it, too, and it's very sad."

Despite her excitement, Lilian forced her expression to remain neutral.

"Could you tell me? I'd much prefer to know the truth about things."

Miss Coates gestured to a seat beside her.

"I used to go to this very same school when I was your age," Miss Coates said, in a soft voice. "A girl called Mary Atkins used to be in my class. Somebody else you may know, too. Ms Strange, the headmistress."

Lilian said nothing, willing Miss Coates to continue.

"I wasn't friends with Mary. Oh, I knew her of course, but I was a bit of a loner back then, preferring the company of books to people." Miss Coates smiled briefly. "Not a lot has changed there."

Lilian leaned forward in her seat.

"I was told that she died during a game of hide-and-seek, is that really true?"

"No, it's not true," Miss Coates said. "And I can't tell you where that rumour came from. But it was a very troubling incident. October half-term was approaching and all the girls, including myself, were very excited. We had a week off school and for many of us, it meant going back home to see our families. I remember Mary holding hands with another girl I hadn't seen before. I only caught a glimpse, but I was struck by how similar she looked to Mary. I assumed it must be her sister, but that's what still gives me the chills even now. Because later, when one of the teachers was looking for Mary to take her on the bus to the train station, I told them what I saw. They said that was impossible, as Mary didn't have a sister. Her family weren't even at the school, they were waiting to pick her up at the station near her home."

"And did they find her...in the wall?"

"They did, but nobody had any idea why she would be in there...unless someone had led her in. But by the time they discovered her it was days later. And too late for Mary, sadly."

A faint creak came from the direction of the door,

making them both jump.

"Just a draught," Miss Coates said, giving Lilian a reassuring smile. "Anyway, where was I?"

Lilian felt she was closer to the truth than ever before. Her skin tingled, her mouth felt dry with anticipation. Gulping, she asked, "So who was the girl you saw her with?"

"I have no idea. I told everyone who asked about my sighting, but nobody was ever able to trace who this mystery girl was. I began to wonder if I'd imagined it. Perhaps I was mistaken. It was a very busy and chaotic day, as you'll find out in a few weeks when your October half-term comes around."

A book fell to the floor with a loud thump. Lilian glanced fearfully at the shelves.

"Don't worry, Lilian, it happens all the time," Miss Coates said. "Too many books, not enough space. But I just want to add that this story about Mary haunting the school, well, I wouldn't waste any more time on it if I were you. Mary was a sweet girl. A very sad girl, too. I remember somebody telling me that her parents had divorced shortly before the incident and I believe she was struggling with her own sadness about her parents' break-up. But I don't believe for one second that she would ever want to frighten anyone. I used to hear some very strange noises here when I was a student, but I didn't see any ghosts. Besides, if the school was really haunted, you only have to look at the history of the place to find more suitable candidates for ghosts than poor Mary."

They were interrupted by the ringing of the library phone.

"I must answer that, excuse me, Lilian."

"But…" Lilian trailed off as Miss Coates disappeared in between the shelves.

You only have to look at the history of the place.

What else had gone on here? Lilian wondered.

It sounded very much like Shadowhall Academy had more secrets to reveal.

Chapter 7

What with everything that had happened, it had been a frenetic first week. The girl behind the wall that Lilian thought she saw, the necklace, the strange story about Cold Mary's disappearance, the hints of other dark secrets buried in the history of Shadowhall Academy. It was all a bit exhausting. Lilian lay in bed and heaved a sigh of relief at not having to get up as early as usual.

It was Sunday morning. Outside, the wind gusted, picking up the loose leaves and hurling them across the grounds in a fit of windy rage. Lilian wriggled her toes and looked around the dormitory. Serena and Angela were chatting quietly on Serena's bed. They seemed to have grown very close in a short time. Marian had yet to surface. All Lilian could see was a tangle of black hair on the pillow.

The only thing they were asked to do on Sundays was attend the morning service in the school chapel. Serena was excused as her family were Hindu, so she'd said she would enjoy an extra snooze in bed and meet them after, but the rest of them were going to go. Lilian had only been to the chapel once. She wasn't sure yet if she believed in God or not, but she enjoyed the dark stillness of the chapel with its smell of candlewax, fresh flowers and the dusty gold-embossed hymn books which felt like something from another time. After the service, they were free to do as they liked, and Lilian ran through the options in her mind. Perhaps today would be a good day to go and see Mr Bullen and ask him about the necklace she'd found? The longer she hung on to it, the guiltier she felt. It might be worth something, or it could be an important historical find. Satisfied with her decision, she went off to brush her teeth.

During the service, Lilian snuck a quick glance at Mr Bullen. He was standing near the front, along with the other teachers, mumbling into his hymn book. Every now and then he seemed to jump a little and stare over his shoulder, as if a cold hand had reached out and touched the back of his neck. He was an odd duck. Lilian got the impression he was scared – but of what? Marian and

Angela stood behind Lilian. When they kneeled for the prayers, Marian leaned forward and whispered in Lilian's ear. "Please God, send us a decent cook."

Which made Lilian want to laugh out loud.

It was as the service was finishing that Lilian noticed something interesting. On the walls of the chapel were memorial plaques. Most were dedicated to former teachers and pupils who had passed on. There was even one dedicated to a former teacher, Ernest Gilbert, who had died in the Second World War and served in the RAF during the Battle of Britain. But the one that caught Lilian's eye looked much older than the others. It was dedicated to a girl called Lucy Groves, and underneath was the date of her birth and death.

1885–1897.

She had only been twelve years old when she died. There was no other information. But this appeared to be the *only* plaque that remembered someone who had nothing to do with the school. Shadowhall hadn't actually been a school back in 1897, Lilian remembered from the brochure. It was curious that there was only one plaque of this kind. Lilian was interrupted by a quiet cough.

"Good morning, Lilian."

Mr Bullen stood at the end of the pew. He attempted what Lilian thought was a smile but it just looked as if he had something unpleasant stuck in his teeth.

"Good morning, sir. Actually there was—"

But Mr Bullen hurried on his way, nodding to the other pupils with an awkward twist of his head.

"I'll see you back at the dormitory," Lilian said, turning round to Marian and Angela.

"Why, what are you up to?" Marian asked.

"I'm going to chat with Mr Bullen about the necklace we found."

"Take some garlic," Marian said with a grin.

"Can't we come, too, Lilian?" Angela asked. "I'd like to know more about that necklace."

Lilian had planned on going on her own, but thinking about it, she wouldn't mind some company down there in the creepy basement. And they had agreed to try and stick together. Maybe all Marian's nudges and winks about Mr Bullen were starting to get to her.

"Okay, let's go."

By the time the girls placed their hymn books back on the tottering pile, Mr Bullen had disappeared. Serena was outside, leaning against the wall with her arms crossed.

"Did I miss anything?" she said.

"No," Lilian said. "But come on, we're on our way to Mr Bullen's office."

"Oh, great, and I thought Sundays were boring," Serena said, sarcastically, but dutifully followed along.

They hurried along the corridor in single file, weaving in and out of the groups of other girls like a snake. Marian led the way, which Lilian was glad about; she was still trying to get to grips with the complex layout of Shadowhall Academy. They descended down a stairwell and past the kitchens, where, by the smell of it, Marian's prayer had yet to be answered.

As before, Lilian felt the atmosphere change down here. It was quieter and darker. The sounds of the school fell away to be replaced by strange creaks and groans from within the walls. The air felt thicker. She found herself glancing over her shoulder, checking to see if Angela and Serena were still in tow.

A moment later, Lilian saw the storeroom they'd tidied up for Ms Strange. Mr Bullen's office was just a little further along. The girls stopped outside his door.

Simon Bullen, History & Antiquities.
Please knock before entering.

"After you," Marian said to Lilian. "You're expedition leader."

Checking the necklace was still in her cardigan pocket, Lilian took a deep breath and knocked. The only answer was silence.

"We must have missed him. Come on, let's go back to bed," Serena said.

"Hang on a sec," Lilian said, before bending the door handle down and pushing it open.

"You can't go in!" Angela hissed.

"It says knock before entering," Lilian replied. "Doesn't say anything about waiting for an answer."

She peered around the door.

It swung open with a slow creak, revealing a small and surprisingly cosy study. There was a large wooden desk, which had been organized in a very neat and tidy way. On one side was a stack of books. On the other, a pile of papers. There was a pen holder, a brass lamp with a green shade, and a large, empty spot right in the middle where somebody could work without having to push things out of the way. Behind the desk was a bookshelf. Next to that, a coffee table with a kettle on it and a teapot. A fire crackled in a large fireplace, in front of which a fireguard had been placed in case any embers were spat out. Lilian was impressed. This was exactly the way she would organize her office…if she had one.

Around the fireplace was a marble engraving of two snakes, which had curled around each other so that their heads were face to face.

"What's that all about?" Lilian whispered to herself. The gargoyle on the gates. The mural of the wolves on the canteen wall. The lions on the staircases. Everything seemed to come in pairs at Shadowhall Academy.

There was nobody to be seen in the study. But then Lilian noticed something odd. Part of the bookshelf appeared to be ajar, as if it was on hinges. Her heart began to beat a little faster, because if she was seeing things correctly, it looked very much like a secret door, concealed within the bookshelf.

Before Lilian had a chance to look closer, she heard the thump of footsteps from behind the bookshelf. Quickly, she darted back outside into the corridor where the others were waiting and closed the office door behind her.

"What's happening?" Marian whispered.

Lilian held a finger to her lips. Seconds later, they heard a dull clunk from inside the office. Lilian waited a few moments and then knocked again. This time, a voice called out.

"Hello there, I'll just…be a moment."

Mr Bullen sounded a little breathless.

"Where did he come from?" Marian whispered.

"There's a secret entrance!" Lilian hissed. "Tell you later."

There were another few clumps and thuds before the door opened a fraction and Mr Bullen's large, watery eyes peered out.

"Oh…um…hello there, what can I do for you?"

"Hello, sir, sorry to bother you," Lilian said. "It's just that we found something we'd like you to take a look at. We think it might be historic."

Mr Bullen's gaze switched from Lilian to Marian, then from Serena to Angela, as if he was weighing up whether this was some kind of trick. Satisfied, he pulled the door open and beckoned them in.

"Well, this is all sounds very intriguing. You best come in and we can take a look together – see if we can't work out what you've unearthed."

The first thing Lilian did was look at the bookshelf. The shelves were all neatly in place, no cracks to be seen. As Mr Bullen went to his desk and took a seat, she noticed he'd left a set of slightly damp footprints behind him. And the last time Lilian had looked, it hadn't been raining.

"Tea?" Mr Bullen said, looking at each of them in turn with raised eyebrows.

"Um…thank you," Lilian said. Really, she wanted to get on with things, but she got the impression that Mr Bullen didn't get many visitors.

They hung around behind his desk as he began a very drawn-out tea-making process. Each cup was placed perfectly in a row, before teabags were delicately placed in the pot, Mr Bullen speaking quietly to himself at every step.

"Now…you go in there…and you go next to him…and then we'll fill you with a little water…and…oops…almost too much…"

On and on it went and Lilian wondered if he knew he was talking out loud. Finally, Mr Bullen poured the hot water in the pot and turned to look at them in surprise, as if he'd quite forgotten that he had company.

"Ah, and now we wait," he said, twisting his fingers together, before beginning to hum again under his breath. Lilian turned slowly to glance at Marian, who flashed her a look of mock horror. Angela stared at the floor, her cheeks blushing a fiery red as she struggled not to giggle. Serena just sighed very loudly.

Finally, cups were handed over and Mr Bullen sat down.

Immediately, he shot up again.

"Biscuits! Girls like biscuits, don't they? Well, I mean, not just because you're girls, because we all like biscuits, don't we? Anyway, I have some somewhere."

Lilian considered herself patient, but this was becoming excruciating, as Mr Bullen proceeded to pull open drawers, and hunt behind books, until he placed a jar on the table.

"There we go, help yourselves."

Each of them politely took one. They were plain and appeared a little past their best, but with Mr Bullen peering across at them, Lilian dutifully took the tiniest bite and forced it down with a sip of Mr Bullen's very strong tea.

"Now then, what do you have for me?" Mr Bullen said.

Retrieving the necklace, Lilian passed it across the table.

Frowning, Mr Bullen picked it up and drew it close to one watery eye.

"This is…*very* interesting," he said quietly.

"It's got an initial inside it, sir," Lilian said. "C."

"Where…what…oh…"

Mr Bullen had gone so pale Lilian thought he might just disappear.

"Is it old?" Marian asked.

"I think it may be," Mr Bullen said, turning it over in hands that appeared to be slightly trembling. "But I would need to check. Do you mind if I keep it for a while?"

"No," Lilian said, Mr Bullen's strange reaction making her wonder if there wasn't more to this necklace than met the eye.

"Do you mind me asking where you found it?"

"In the—"

"In the grounds," Marian said, cutting Lilian off before she could mention they'd been inside the wall looking for a ghost. "We were just walking along, minding our business, and Lilian spotted it in the bushes."

"Curious," Mr Bullen said. "It seems very well-preserved for something that's been out in the elements. I would have expected much more obvious signs of wear and tear." He looked up at them. "I shall report back once I've confirmed my suspicions. Perhaps you can give me a few days. Is there anything else I can help with?"

"No, thanks, sir," Marian said.

"Thank you," Angela said.

Lilian had a think. She had so many questions about Shadowhall Academy rattling around in her brain, it seemed too good an opportunity to give up.

"There is one thing," Lilian said. "I spotted a memorial plaque in the chapel today. It was for a girl called Lucy Groves. I just wondered if you knew who she was?"

"What was that?" Mr Bullen said. His attention had returned to the necklace.

"There's a memorial plaque in the chapel, sir," Lilian repeated. "For someone called Lucy Groves. I wondered if you knew anything more about her?"

"Why that one in particular?" Mr Bullen asked, his eyes narrowing.

"It's older than all the others," Lilian replied. "And she was around the same age as me...when she died. I wondered what happened to her."

"Ah, yes... She was a housemaid to the family that owned the estate, the Boulogne family. Before Shadowhall Academy, this house and grounds were in their possession for centuries. Lucy Groves's story was a sad one. After both her parents died of typhoid, she was forced to enter service as a means to survive, but alas, she went missing after only a few months. There were a lot of conflicting accounts surrounding the exact circumstances of her disappearance, but one thing wasn't in question – she was never seen again."

Lilian's ears pricked up. Even Serena sat back down.

"So, what happened?" Lilian asked. "I mean, you can't just disappear, can you?"

"Maybe she decided she'd had enough of being a servant," Marian sniffed.

"It was certainly very mysterious," Mr Bullen said, his eyes returning to the necklace. "Well, I'll get back to you about this find of yours shortly but please feel free to visit me again. It's a pleasure to be in the company of curious minds."

The girls began to get up and walk towards the door. But Lilian wasn't finished asking questions. Just before they exited, she turned.

"Sir, what was so mysterious about Lucy Groves's disappearance? I mean, she might have just run away?"

Mr Bullen looked up at her.

"It's possible. The reason why it was considered so puzzling is that another servant reported seeing her with another girl shortly before her disappearance. Someone who was said to resemble her, almost to the point of being an exact double. The servant assumed it was Lucy's sister. But Lucy Groves was an only child."

Chapter 8

Lilian woke on Monday morning to find that her brain had already switched itself on. She hadn't even opened her eyes properly before dark theories swirled around her mind.

The first girl she'd learned about was Mary Atkins. Then there was Lucy Groves. Both gone missing in mysterious circumstances that involved someone seeing an almost exact double of them right before they were last seen alive. One was mysterious enough. But what were the chances of two identical incidents happening in exactly the same place?

Lilian had discussed it with the other girls on their way back from Mr Bullen's office, telling them what Miss Coates had told her about Cold Mary and the similarities to Lucy Groves's disappearance. All of them agreed that it was highly unsettling. Even Serena could only offer a shrug – and Serena normally had an answer for everything. Also, why did Mr Bullen have a door hidden in his bookshelf? And where did it lead?

Thinking about secret entrances, Lilian's gaze was drawn to the hatch above Angela's bed. It was covered now but still she imagined a pale face behind it, staring back at her. There hadn't been any knocking since Angela's first night, but Lilian couldn't forget what she'd heard – and later seen – in there.

She was sure there was a link between Mary Atkins and Lucy Groves.

But what exactly was it?

Lilian knew she had to try and find out. It was like having an itch in the middle of your back that you couldn't quite reach. You had to do something about it. You just weren't sure how and ended up tying yourself in knots.

All Lilian knew for sure was that the answer lay somewhere in the past.

Somewhere in Shadowhall Academy's dark history, there were answers to be found.

Lilian swept up all the random thoughts that swirled around her head and packed them neatly away for later.

Because right now, there was a more pressing challenge.

Not only was it Monday, universally agreed to be the worst day of the week, but this morning they were going to do a cross-country run. Lilian had never done one before and she felt fraught with nerves. She never really did any exercise and remembered the girls she'd seen running when she first arrived. They'd looked so fit and strong. Lilian wondered if she might just keel over halfway through. Perhaps they'd find her, white and stiff, lying in the grass with bloodshot eyes, one hand pressed over her heart, and a look of horror on her face.

Climbing out of bed, she pulled the curtains apart. The rain left grey streaks on the windows. Beyond, the treetops swayed in the strong gusts. Red and orange leaves swirled in the air like bonfire embers. This wasn't running outside weather, Lilian thought. It wasn't even walking, sitting, or standing outside weather. This was a day made for books and blankets, tea and biscuits.

Serena walked past with sleepy eyes on her way to the bathroom.

"Ahoy there," she mumbled.

"Um, Serena, do you think they'll cancel the cross-country?" Lilian asked, turning to gaze back out of the window. "The weather looks terrible."

Serena laughed loudly, as if this was the most absurd suggestion she'd ever heard.

"Oh, dear Lilian, you've so much to learn about Shadowhall, including the fact that there's more chance of them turning up the heating than cancelling the running. Even if the next ice age began, we'd all still be out there, puffing our way past the woolly mammoths. The only way you're getting out of this is if the world suddenly decides to end before 9.30 a.m."

Lilian shivered and climbed back into bed, but it wasn't the same. The warmth had left the bedclothes. She knew she was only delaying the inevitable, so she went and joined Serena and the other girls in the bathroom.

True to Serena's word, after breakfast, Lilian found herself standing shivering in the rain alongside her equally miserable-looking room-mates. She'd been handed a navy and gold running kit, but it seemed to have been made for someone much bigger and hung off her bony shoulders like something a scarecrow would wear. She looked like a very disappointing imitation of the girls she'd seen on her first day.

"I don't really do running," Lilian said to Angela. "You?"

Angela forced a weak smile.

"I ran after a bus once, does that count?"

Marian came to join them. Her spiky hair had been flattened by the wind and rain and she had to tug the wet strands out of her eyes.

"Ready to experience hell on earth?" she said, her knees already raw and chapped.

The girls lined up. A few of the more athletic ones made their way to the front and leaned forward, hands on knees, eyes focused straight ahead, as if this was the final of some Olympic event. But Lilian was relieved to see that they were in the minority and most of the girls looked like they were already on their last legs before the run had even begun.

"Right then, girls," shouted the PE teacher Miss Pine, who appeared to be incapable of talking at normal volume and had the same build as a heavyweight boxer, her shoulders protruding through the sleeves of her tracksuit top. "Stick to the route. Maintain a steady pace. Keep your breathing even. Don't give up. Focus. And remember, fatigue is all in the mind!"

Lilian thought they were just going for a run. This was beginning to sound like a battle to the death. She took a deep breath as Miss Pine raised a whistle to her mouth before blowing an ear-splitting shriek.

"Away you go!" bellowed Miss Pine.

And away they went.

After what only seemed like a few seconds, Lilian's lungs felt like flat tyres and she struggled to draw in enough air. They appeared to be running directly into the wind, so it felt like she had to run doubly hard just to keep moving forward. The rain on her skin was like being pelted with pebbles. Serena pulled ahead, while Lilian, Marian and Angela were all towards the back of the pack. They headed across the lawn at the front of the school, before turning to the left and down towards the shore of the lake. Lilian found herself distracted as the strange domed monument on the island came into view. She remembered seeing it on the day she arrived. Slowing her pace, she let the others pass on by. Most of the building was obscured by tall reeds, but it had a gloomy appearance that made Lilian wrinkle her nose with curiosity. Marian had briefly mentioned that it was out of bounds, but there was a small boat, tethered to the shore, which suggested someone was visiting it. Perhaps this was something else she needed to find out more about. She added it to her already long list of *things-to-be-investigated-further.*

Glancing up, Lilian noticed that she'd fallen behind the rest of the girls. She could just about see the back of

Angela's head in the distance, maybe a windswept ball of black hair that could be Marian. While she had dawdled, everyone else had passed the lake and was following a trail that led them into the woods. While she was sure that most of the girls knew the route well, Lilian didn't, and so she forced her gaze away from the lake and its mysterious building and turned back into the wind, grimacing as a fierce gust squeezed tears from her eyes. As the trail led her up a slight incline, Lilian's legs stiffened, like matchsticks, and her ankle began to ache. It didn't bode well for the rest of the run. She certainly wouldn't be pushing for first place. But she didn't want to come last either, and so she gulped down more air, bent her head, and tried to ignore the discomfort and get herself into a rhythm.

The grass grew longer as she left the well-tended grounds, and as she reached the tree canopy, the day darkened even further, and she found herself swallowed up by the gloom of the wood. Twigs cracked underfoot and she had to keep her eyes peeled to avoid being tripped by the roots and fallen logs that occasionally strayed into her path. While she couldn't see anyone else on the snaking trail, up ahead she could hear the occasional shout and whoop. But as she continued running, the atmosphere began to change. The voices faded into silence. The wind hissed menacingly through the treetops. The trail grew less defined and harder to see, and Lilian found herself having to double back as she ran into a clump of bushes. With a small flutter of panic in her belly, Lilian realized that she'd lost her bearings. As she attempted to get back on track, she became aware that somebody was watching her.

Out of the corner of her eye, she could see someone standing way off in the trees.

Lilian slowed to a halt.

It appeared to be a girl around her age, but she was too far away to make out much else. Her face was swathed in shadows. All Lilian could tell was that the girl appeared to have very pale skin and long, fairish hair. The girl wasn't wearing the navy and gold running kit they all had, either. She was wearing an old-fashioned dress of some kind, which looked strangely out of place on this wet and windy autumn day. Lilian wondered if maybe it was a costume for a theatre production or something. If so, she'd chosen the wrong day to go for a walk through the woods in it.

"Hello!" Lilian cried, but it came out as a strangled gasp and so she tried again. "Hey, sorry, but do you know where the running trail is?"

The girl's head angled slightly, but she made no response and simply continued to stare. Lilian wondered if maybe the girl couldn't hear her very well. It was really windy and the rustle of the branches overhead sounded like waves sweeping up a pebbled beach. Lilian cupped her hands around her mouth.

"Hello, can you hear me?"

The girl made no movement nor gave any acknowledgement. It was beginning to unnerve Lilian a little. Even if she couldn't be heard, it was obvious from her movements that she was attempting to communicate. Yet the girl remained as stiff as a statue. Lilian picked her way through the ferns, trying to get closer.

She waved her hands.

"Hello there! I think I'm lost, can you help?"

Lilian was too far away to make out whether there was any change in the girl's expression, but surely she could see her waving? Lilian didn't know whether to be annoyed or scared. The girl's behaviour wasn't natural. Lilian felt as if she was being assessed.

"All I want are some directions," Lilian called.

Once again, Lilian tried to close the distance between them. Now she was firmly mired in the undergrowth and her feet were catching on vines and foliage. Twice she nearly fell. There was no sign of any trail.

"Hey, can you just help me?" Lilian called again.

But when she looked up for an answer, the girl had disappeared.

She had been standing there just a second ago and now all Lilian could see were trees.

Shivering, she wondered where the girl had gone.

And more importantly, why had she just stood and stared?

Lilian tried to extricate herself from the boggy undergrowth, feeling her knees and shins getting sodden and chafed as they snagged on the sharp ends of twigs. She slipped on a mossy log and felt her ankle twist. The next thing she knew she was lying on her back, feeling the clammy leaves press into her spine.

Lilian groaned.

At that moment, a cold, high, clear laugh rang out through the woods.

A girl's laugh.

Lilian called out. "I need help! I think I've twisted my ankle!"

She raised her head and looked around but there was nobody to be seen.

Lilian shuddered. A few seconds ago, her skin had

been cold and wet. Now it felt as if the chill had burrowed down into her bones.

Because it very much sounded as if someone was laughing *at her.*

Chapter 9

Lilian sat on the wet ground, trying to understand what had just happened. She'd fallen, was freezing to death, had possibly injured her leg, and all the strange girl could do was laugh.

It was horrible and it was sinister.

Tentatively, she wiggled her ankle. It moved from side to side, like ankles are supposed to, and while it was still sore, she considered that to be a good sign.

Considering whether to try standing on it, she heard a voice calling out from behind her.

"Lilian? Can you hear me? Are you in here?"

Relief flooded through Lilian as if a hot tap had just been turned on. It was Marian.

"I'm over here!" Lilian called back.

Lilian raised herself on her elbows and saw Marian jogging towards her through the rain.

"Are you okay?" Marian said. "Have you hurt yourself?"

"No," Lilian said, miserably. "Well, I mean, yes, I did fall over, but I think I'm okay. I thought I'd twisted my ankle, but it seems to be working."

"Want to give it a try?" Marian said, holding out her hand for Lilian to take.

"Okay."

Lilian let Marian help her up. Tentatively, she wiggled her ankle again. The pain was fading.

"I wondered where you got to," Marian said. "I came back just in case you'd drowned in the lake and had gone to live in the wall with Cold Mary."

"It's not quite that dramatic," Lilian said. "Though something really weird did just happen."

Despite her bedraggled appearance, Marian's eyes shone. "Tell me more."

"There was a girl, here in the woods. I called out to her because I was lost and thought she might point me in the right direction. Then I fell on my ankle. This girl though, she didn't say anything. Didn't help me. Just stood there and stared. She even laughed when she saw me fall over... Well, I heard someone laughing and she was the only other person here."

"What did she look like?" Marian asked. "I thought it was only us poor runners who were out in the woods."

"Um…well…I couldn't make out too much detail, but she was wearing this really odd dress, like Alice in Wonderland or something. She wasn't on a cross-country run, that's for certain."

"Hmm," Marian said. "That is weird. Pretty rotten thing to do too, just ignore you. Maybe she was only messing with you and didn't realize you'd hurt yourself?"

"Well, I told her," Lilian said. "She gave me a bad feeling."

"Not everyone here is as nice as me, you know," Marian said, with a smile. "How's your leg? Can you jog on it?"

"Yes, I think so," Lilian said, rotating her ankle in gentle circles. "But we're so far behind now, we'll never catch up."

"Not if we run the official route," Marian said. "Luckily for us, I know a shortcut. Come on."

Marian led them off through the woods, then darted down along a narrow trail that Lilian wouldn't ever have noticed. Leaves scattered down into their path. The branches dripped overhead, flicking cold little shocks onto the backs of their necks. Now that the adrenalin had worn off, Lilian was beginning to feel stiff and chilly again and her ankle still felt sore. She couldn't resist darting glances left and right, curious to see if the mysterious girl reappeared, but apart from a furious clamour of rooks, they appeared to be the only ones there. After about ten minutes of silent, sodden marching, Marian paused as she reached the edge of the wood.

"Not many girls mind if you take a shortcut," Marian whispered at her shoulder. "But there's a few that won't hesitate dobbing you in to Miss Pine if they see you. I think the coast is clear, come on."

Darting out of the wood, they found the running trail and it wasn't long before they could see a few stragglers at the back.

"Look, there's Angela," Marian panted. "Let's catch her up."

They drew up alongside Angela, who gave them both a surprised look.

"Where did you two appear from?"

"Lilian got lost in the woods and I bravely went to rescue her," Marian said.

"You got lost in the woods?" Angela echoed, that fearful look immediately back on her face.

"No, not really, I just got into a bit of a scrape," Lilian said. "I'll tell you later."

Thankfully, it wasn't long before the turrets of Shadowhall Academy came into view, and they found themselves running back through the grounds. Miss Pine stood on what was probably supposed to be a finish line, clapping her hands like an enthusiastic seal.

"Well done, girls! Keep it up, you're nearly there!" she cried. "Train through the pain!"

And then, mercifully, the run was over. Lilian rested her hands on her knees and waited for her breathing to slow. Marian and Angela did the same, their cheeks red, their brows shiny with sweat. A chill wind blew through their wet hair. Lilian noticed that some of the girls who'd finished first were already making their way back to the changing rooms. Serena came to join them, looking as if she'd just popped out for a brief stroll.

"Well, I don't remember seeing any of you out enjoying the fresh air. Did Maz show you her shortcut?"

"What short cut?" Angela said, looking at Lilian and Marian with a hurt expression.

"Yes, I did," Marian replied. "But only because Lilian got lost and injured in the woods."

Serena bent her head to one side and half-smiled, half-frowned.

"You got lost?"

"Long story," Lilian gasped, trying to get her breath back. "I'll tell you later…when I can get a sentence out… without dying."

After showering and getting changed back into their school uniforms, Lilian really wanted to spend the rest of the day in bed with a book, but Shadowhall Academy had other plans. These involved chemistry, English language, English literature, French and religious studies. Lilian yawned through most of them and finally, thankfully, there was only history left with Mr Bullen. After class had finished and they were tidying away their books, he shuffled towards Lilian and the girls.

"Stakes at the ready," Marian whispered.

"I have news," he announced. They must have looked confused because he added hurriedly, "about the necklace."

"That's great, sir!" Lilian exclaimed, her tiredness suddenly falling away from her.

"Is it historic then?" Angela said.

"Is it valuable?" Serena added.

"It is historic, I'm ninety-nine per cent certain," Mr Bullen said, twisting his hands together. Lilian thought he almost looked excited. "As for its value, while I don't think it would set any records at auction, it's certainly very valuable to a historian of this property, like myself."

"Oh," Serena said, with a disappointed expression.

"Best of all," Mr Bullen said, "if you care to accompany me, I can tell you more about the history of Shadowhall and who might have owned a necklace like that!" He clapped his hands together. "If you have a few minutes, we could go and have a look right now."

Lilian was excited to see what Mr Bullen had in store. It seemed the necklace was too old to belong to Cold Mary, so what was it doing in the wall? She hurriedly finished stuffing her books in her bag. The others followed suit and they followed Mr Bullen out of the classroom and along a corridor, then back down to the basement.

But Mr Bullen wasn't leading them to his office. Instead, he walked past it, past the storeroom where they'd found the photograph of Mary Atkins, and along a little further until he produced a key from his jacket pocket and unlocked a door marked *PRIVATE*.

"This is what I like to call the artefact room," he said, ushering them inside. "There are still some items left over from when the school was a private residence. I don't know why they haven't been sold or ended up in a museum yet, but it's lucky for us. I'm in the process of cataloguing everything but it takes time, a resource which I have little of, being so busy with you and your peers."

It was one of those rooms that was larger on the inside than it looked from the outside, like Doctor Who's TARDIS. There were lots of wooden crates, and Lilian could see the outlines of a few chairs and chests, covered with white cloths to protect them. They all crowded in and looked expectantly at Mr Bullen. He stood in front of what appeared to be a painting. One corner of the white sheet that covered it had fallen off and Lilian could just make out the edge of a faded and ornate bronze frame.

"Now then," Mr Bullen said, with the air of a magician about to produce a rabbit from a hat. "Allow me to introduce someone who may have touched the very necklace you found."

He drew back the sheet, which tumbled to the ground with a soft hiss, like a deflating ghost.

It took Lilian a few seconds to work out what she was seeing.

It was a portrait of a young girl. She had long reddish hair and wore a puffy blue dress which billowed out from the waist. Her eyes were black and unnaturally large, almost as if the painter had made a mistake. Lilian had never seen eyes that huge before. She looked out at the viewer with a slight frown, her mouth parted, as if she might be about to cry out.

But there was something else in the painting, too.

Some*one* else.

Behind the girl lurked another figure, dressed in an identical blue dress, with the same long hair that was the colour of an autumn sunset. With one hand, the figure behind had reached out to grasp the girl by the shoulder, as if they were about to spin her around.

Only, the figure in the background had something very different about it.

In place of a face, there was a skull.

"Who is she, sir?" Lilian whispered with a shiver. The girl seemed strangely familiar.

"Her name is Isobel Boulogne and she lived here nearly one hundred and fifty years ago, back before Shadowhall Academy became the school we all know and love."

Serena snorted into her sleeve, but Mr Bullen pretended not to hear.

"This building, as I previously mentioned, was the ancestral home of the Boulogne family. They have a long lineage, dating all the way back to when Gilbert Boulogne came over from France with William the Conqueror, to do battle with King Harold II in 1066. Gilbert was gifted this estate by the Conqueror himself, as a reward for his loyal service. Gilbert's descendants lived here for many hundreds of years until a member of their family bequeathed the building to a charity, after which, it became our school. You'll no doubt have seen the family mausoleum on the island. Many of them are buried there, Isobel included, though it's strictly out-of-bounds of course."

A mausoleum.

The breath rushed out of Lilian's body.

So that's what the mysterious building was – the one she'd stopped to study during her cross-country run. She knew at that moment she simply had to see it up close. But she focused her attention back on Mr Bullen, who was fiddling with his shirt cuffs.

"Why did they paint her like that?" Lilian said. "With the skull girl in the background?"

"Isobel died at a young age," Mr Bullen said. "The figure behind her is meant to represent Death, I believe. Children dying wasn't as unusual back then as it is now. Our ancestors lived side by side with their own mortality in a way that we can't really understand today. And while this portrait may look very sinister to our modern gaze, I don't believe it would have been seen that way in the past. Simply a symbolic reminder that death is never far away."

"Skeleton girls!" Marian whispered in Lilian's ear. "This is better than I thought."

Mr Bullen fell silent, staring at the painting as if hypnotized. It *was* hard to take your eyes away, even though it seemed to make the temperature in the room even colder.

"But why are they dressed the same?" Lilian asked. "Shouldn't Death be wearing a black shroud and carrying a scythe or something?"

Bending down, Mr Bullen rearranged the sheet back over the painting.

"As I say, it's very much a product of its time."

"So, who's C then?" Angela asked in a small voice.

Mr Bullen frowned and raised a long, slender finger. "C?"

"The initial on the necklace," Angela said, pushing her glasses back on the bridge of her nose. "If this girl is called Isobel, then it's not her necklace, is it?"

Mr Bullen coughed and ran a hand through his hair.

"No, I simply wanted to show you someone who lived around the time the necklace was made," he stammered. "As for who C was, I expect that shall remain a mystery. Anyway, I'll let you get back to your dormitory now, it's nearly dinner time." He rummaged in his pocket and pulled out the necklace. "Here, Lilian, why don't you keep hold of this until I find a suitable home for it."

"Thank you, sir, I'll look after it," Lilian said. As she closed her fingers around the necklace, she had a strange urge to look at the painting again, but Mr Bullen had covered it up.

"And remember," he said. "Don't let the painting disturb you, it's just one artist's rather dark imagination."

Despite his words of comfort, Lilian was left with a very unsettling feeling.

Because the girl in the painting reminded her very much of the girl she'd seen in the woods.

Chapter 10

By the time they'd finished supper, Lilian could barely make her way upstairs to the dorm room, each step making her bruised ankle ache even more. It felt like it had been the longest day ever. She brushed her teeth as quickly as she could, hurried to the dorm, pulled back the sheets, said goodnight to Ms Strange when she popped in for lights out, then stretched out her legs with a long, satisfied sigh. Even her ironing board mattress felt comfy tonight.

Lilian fell into a sleep that was punctuated by sinister dreams of girls with swirling red hair, black eyes and piercing laughs. She woke at some point in the night to the sound of rustling coming from Angela's bed. Squinting through one sleepy eye, she could see Angela getting up and pulling on her dressing gown, before sliding her feet into her slippers. Then, strangely, she slipped her coat on. Must be colder than usual in the loo, Lilian thought, before plonking her head back down on her pillow.

Yet she didn't fall straight back to sleep. The wind whooshed and whistled, making huge great sighs and groans as it rattled the windows in their frames. Lilian felt unsettled. She raised herself on one elbow and looked over at Marian's bed.

"Maz?" she whispered. "You awake?"

The only answer was soft, even breaths.

Lilian wanted company. She sensed that something wasn't quite right. And Angela hadn't returned yet.

Levering herself up out of bed, Lilian snatched her dressing gown and quickly pulled it on. Her feet searched in the dark for her slippers and with a backwards glance at Marian and Serena, she quietly opened the door and walked to the bathroom.

"Angela?" she called.

There was a faint smell of toothpaste in the air. A tap dripped, adding a melancholy sound. It was creepy in there, but Lilian could tell it was empty. Even so, she checked all the cubicles, just in case.

But where could Angela have gone?

Poking her head out of the bathroom door, Lilian peered up and down the corridor. It was empty and silent. Tentatively, she made her way back to the dormitory. Opening the door, she saw that Angela's bed was still empty. Lilian was getting worried now. She tiptoed over to Marian's bed.

"Maz… Marian," she whispered. "Are you awake?"

All she got in reply was a groan.

Lilian pulled back one of the heavy curtains and peered out. The rain hadn't eased. She could still see it slanting down in the beam from one of the school's powerful spotlights. She saw something else, too. Just for a moment. Two small figures making their way across the grass.

Towards the lake.

Even though she was walking away from the school, with her back to her, Lilian instantly knew that one of them was Angela.

She dashed out through the door and down the stairs, not caring if anyone heard her. Angela wouldn't be wandering outside at night unless something was wrong. Reaching the entrance hall, Lilian ran to the main doors, noticing they'd been unlocked. One swung open in the breeze and Lilian grasped the handle and tugged it the rest of the way. The rain pecked at her eyes, forcing her to squint. The wind lifted her hair with invisible fingers. Her dressing gown did little to keep the cold out, but she pulled it tighter all the same.

In the distance, Lilian could just about make out Angela, holding hands with another girl. They were both dressed in hooded jackets and walking very slowly. Lilian wondered if Angela was sleepwalking. Her sister, Susan, had gone through a sleepwalking phase when she was young, and they'd found her wandering around the garden in her PJs more than once.

But who was the other girl?

Lilian sprinted towards them, swiping her wet hair out of her eyes.

For a moment, as Lilian ran into a dip on the grass, she lost sight of them. When she saw them again, they were close to the shore of the lake. The pounding rain made the surface of the lake resemble a pan of boiling water.

"Angela!" Lilian cried.

The two girls stopped. Angela turned, blinking, as if waking from a dream. Then she glanced at the girl beside her, as if seeing her for the first time. With a look of shock, Angela tried to free her hand from the girl's grip, but she held on tightly before trying to tug Angela away.

"Hey, you leave her alone!" Lilian shouted.

As she closed the gap between them, the unknown girl released Angela's hand, turned once to dart a glance at Lilian, then ran off into the misty rain.

Lilian reached Angela and wrapped her up in a hug. She couldn't say any words of comfort at first. Her heart felt like it had leaped into her throat. Every hair on her head felt stiff and brittle, as if they were made of ice. She couldn't be sure of what she'd seen; the rain was falling, she'd been running, her hair was in her eyes.

Yet for a moment, when the girl had turned briefly, she had looked like the spitting image of Angela herself.

"Who was she?" Lilian gasped, as she led Angela back towards the school.

"I d-don't know," Angela said. "I thought I was dreaming."

"I saw you leave the room. I thought you were going to the loo."

Angela screwed up her face in confusion. "I...could hear a voice, telling me I had to go outside, because you were all waiting for me there."

"Us?" Lilian stopped in her tracks. "But we were all in bed!"

"You were?" Angela said. "But when I looked, your beds were all empty?"

Lilian shook her head. She'd never heard of any sleepwalking like this before.

"Go on," Lilian said.

"When I got to the main door, I pushed it open, and there was a girl waiting for me. She said I had to come quickly because Marian was in trouble and needed my help. Her voice sounded so familiar. Like she was someone I knew. So we started walking and she gripped my hand but hers felt so cold. I kept trying to look at her, but I couldn't see her face because of her hood. And I noticed she had the same coat as me, which was weird. I asked her name, but she didn't reply. Then I started to get soaking wet in the rain and I realized it wasn't a dream at all. When I heard you call my name it was like someone set off an alarm clock."

Lilian shivered. It was one of the most unsettling incidents she'd ever experienced.

"Let's get back inside," she said. "We're like a couple of drowned rats."

As they neared the main doors, a dark shadow flitted across the light like a giant bat.

Lilian tugged Angela towards the bushes, where the

light didn't reach. They held their breath. The door squealed on its hinges as it was pushed open. Mr Bullen emerged and stood at the top of the steps with a torch. As he shone it around, Lilian and Angela shrank further back in the bushes. Mr Bullen breathed in, deeply inhaling the night air. Then, much to Lilian and Angela's relief, he opened an umbrella, walked down the steps and set off across the fields – in the same direction the girl had gone.

"Quick," Lilian hissed. "Let's get inside."

They ran up the stairs and into the hallway, their wet clothes leaving a dripping trail of guilt behind them.

"Thank you for coming after me," Angela whispered, once they were safely back in the dormitory and drying off their hair. "Who was she, do you think, the girl outside?"

"I'm working on that," Lilian said. "It's all very strange."

"What's strange is you two running around outside at night," Serena said, sitting up in bed. "But I must admit, Lilian, I'm impressed by your determination to get slung out of this school."

"Uh-oh, what's happened now?" Marian said sleepily, raising her head off the pillow and scratching her head.

Lilian and Angela told them what had just transpired, out in the rainy night.

"And you don't know who this girl is?" Serena asked. "Seems odd that she'd be waiting for you outside?"

"Not if she wasn't…a normal girl," Lilian said quietly.

Serena got up, grabbed something from underneath the bed, then plonked herself down on Lilian's bed and produced a biscuit tin from behind her back.

"I have in my possession, courtesy of my mother, golden crunch creams, malted milks, Jaffa Cakes, Penguins, Bourbons and pink wafers. This sounds like a chat that's going to need a lot of biscuits."

With that, she popped open the lid and rattled the inside, which was nearly overflowing with everything crunchy, crispy and gooey in biscuit form. It was like a scene from Charlie and the Chocolate Factory.

"I need one of those," Marian said, coming to join Serena. "Angela, I think you could do with one, too, after that horrible experience."

Angela put down the towel that she'd been using to dry her hair. Serena shook the biscuit tin in her direction. A few moments later, and all four of them were munching away, wrapped up in a cosy pile of eiderdowns, blankets and pillows.

Serena narrowed her eyes. "So, who was the girl with Angela?" she said. "And what did she want? That's so freaky."

"That's not even the strangest thing," Lilian said. "Angela, the girl you were with...she looked just like you."

Lilian caught a glimpse of Angela's pale face and wide eyes.

"But...how could that be?" Angela said.

"Don't you see?" Lilian said. "Mary Atkins disappears with someone who looked just like her. Before that, Lucy Groves, that servant Mr Bullen told us about, disappears with someone who looked just like her, too. And now this. I mean, you don't have to be Sherlock Holmes to see a connection."

Lilian leaned back on her pillows. It felt as if they were coming closer to something she wasn't sure she wanted to know.

"Also, there was that painting today," Marian said. "Weird how the girl with the skull was dressed just like Isobel Boulogne. Same dress. Same hair, too."

"You know, Isobel is buried in the family mausoleum on the island," Lilian added. "Mr Bullen said so. Angela was heading in that direction when I found her."

"Uh-oh, I know where this is going," Serena said.

"I think we need to go and find her grave," Lilian said.

"And there we have it," Serena said with a grimace. "At least Marian will enjoy it. Graveyards are your specialist subject, aren't they, Spooky?"

"I would be interested, you are indeed correct," Marian said, her pale face peeking out from a nest of pillows. "But it's out of bounds."

"Why would you want to go and look at Isobel's grave?" Angela said, taking a dainty nibble of her pink wafer.

"Because it's a daring escapade," Serena said. "It's forbidden. And it's dangerous. There's three good reasons for you."

"I want to find out more about Isobel and how she died," Lilian added. "There's something else I haven't told you. I can't get it out of my mind. The girl in the woods. I swear it was the same girl in the painting. Red hair. Blue dress. Big, dark eyes. She was a little way off but when I saw that painting, I swear…"

Lilian trailed off.

The girls all looked at one another.

"That's…impossible though," Serena said, eventually.

"It's as impossible as Mary Atkins knocking on the wall," Marian said. "And that happened."

"We don't know that," Serena said.

"We *do*," Marian muttered to herself.

"At least if we go to the mausoleum we might find out more about Isobel," Lilian said. "I don't know about you lot but something about all this feels off to me. Like there's something we don't know but we need to."

"I don't want to get in trouble again," Angela said. "I've only just started here."

"You won't get in trouble," Serena said. "Because nobody will see us. But if you don't want to come, that's fine, you can stay here and hold the fort…on your own."

Lilian could sense Angela's fear rise into the air.

"Okay, well, maybe I'll come, too," Angela said. "As long as we don't get caught."

Serena crossed her fingers. "I promise to take personal responsibility for keeping you hidden from the watchful eyes of Ms Strange. When do you want to go, Lilian?"

Lilian hadn't prepared for this. She'd only got so far as deciding she wanted to go. In some respects, it felt like Serena had called her bluff. She couldn't back out now though. Swallowing hard, she gave it a moment's thought.

"Well, how about this weekend? Some of the teachers won't be around and the day girls will all be at home, too. There'll be less chance of us getting spotted."

"Sometime in the afternoon?" Marian suggested.

Serena cut in. "No, there's still too many people around in the daytime. We'll go at night. After lights out."

Chapter 11

As the rest of the week passed, Lilian became increasingly nervous. Not just about their trip to the mausoleum. She found herself listening for noises at night. Doing double takes at every red-headed girl she passed. Wondering what name C could stand for.

They'd started taking steps at night to make sure Angela didn't get lured out of the dorm again – and that nobody could get in without them knowing. After lights out, the girls would get out of bed and pile pillows and cushions and blankets against the door, before gently balancing old biscuit tins on top and pushing forks, knives and spoons into the crevices. It was like an alarm system. One false move and there would be a deafening clatter.

Lilian did want to see the mausoleum. Partly from

curiosity, but mainly because she just had an instinct that there might be something in Isobel's tomb that could help them piece things together – maybe clues as to how Isobel died. Was she another girl that was last seen with someone who looked like her? Lilian wasn't sure how she would find this information exactly, but she knew that sometimes the cause of death was written on tombstones. If Isobel had died of an illness or something, then Lilian would know that Isobel's case wasn't connected to the other girls.

The one thing above all else, Lilian told herself, was making sure they weren't caught. The thought of being called into Ms Strange's office again and being fixed with those cold, grey eyes made her shudder. Serena's fearless attitude worried her a little. She didn't seem to worry about precautions. Marian, she could rely on. Angela? She was the one that gave Lilian the most concern. She would be terrified before they'd even set foot outside the door. And what would happen if she got Angela into trouble? Lilian would never forgive herself. She resolved to try and talk Angela out of coming. She would be safer and happier staying in the dormitory, even if it meant she would be alone.

These worries circled endlessly around Lilian's head

like a flock of vultures, but Saturday arrived and she knew that it was too late to back out now. Serena had found them more torches. Marian had prepared a slightly odd backpack containing a pack of biscuits, an umbrella, and a fancy new Polaroid camera that her parents had given her. It was easy to use. You just snapped the picture and the photograph slid out of the bottom a few moments later. Marian said it had a flash so they could take pictures of the gravestones even in the dark.

Everyone appeared ready and eager to go.

In the afternoon, they gathered outside on the lawn to make their final plans for the evening.

"So what time are we doing this?" Marian said, excitedly.

"Lights out is at nine," Serena said. "I think we should wait at least an hour, you know, give everyone time to get to their beds and fall asleep."

"The boat is still in the same place by the lake," Lilian said. "I checked earlier."

"Looks like it might be a cold night," Angela said, staring up at the darkening blue sky, a sharp sliver of silver moon already visible on the horizon.

Lilian took her chance.

"You know, it might be better if you stay, Angela. We

need a lookout back at the base. You can flash the torch in the window when we return, let us know that the coast is clear."

Angela's lower lip trembled. "You don't want me to come?"

"Oh no," Lilian said. "Not that at all. I just thought, you know, you might prefer it. It is going to be pretty chilly by the looks of it. And it might be a little scary, too."

"I'm not staying on my own...in *that* room," Angela said. "That's way scarier."

"We stick together then," Serena said. "As we agreed."

Lilian wasn't happy about the Angela situation, but she did have a point: their dorm room wasn't the best place to be left alone. Not after everything that had happened. And so she nodded.

"Okay, so we go tonight, after lights out," Lilian said. "All of us."

The rest of the evening involved watching the clock and trying to banish thoughts of angry teachers catching them red-handed. Lilian felt her excitement growing, too. She was desperate to find answers to a mystery that had been unsolved for hundreds of years. It was also beginning to feel as if she'd met a group of girls with whom anything was possible. Serena had guts. Marian had guile. Even

Angela had a toughness to her that Lilian hadn't realized. She made a silent promise never to try and exclude Angela again. She was one of them.

After dinner, Lilian examined her wardrobe through narrowed eyes, before selecting what she thought was the best outfit for the night ahead. Jeans, a heavy woolly jumper, waterproof jacket, bobble hat, thick socks and ankle boots. The others did the same. With lights out fast approaching, they changed into their outdoor clothes, before jumping into bed for the teachers' nightly inspection. Being in bed made Lilian feel warm and cosy. She could sense the dark night pressing its cold hands against the window. Maybe it would be better if they all just stayed in bed instead?

Tonight, it was Mr Bullen who stuck his head around the door.

"Good evening," he said, before pausing to glance over his shoulder, his eyes narrowing as if he'd heard something. After a few moments, he turned back towards them. "It's time for lights out I believe, girls. Sleep well."

"Goodnight, sir," they all said in their cheeriest, we're-not-doing-anything-wrong voices.

Five minutes later, they were lacing their boots and checking supplies, before huddling nervously together on

Lilian's bed. Even Serena nibbled her nails as she checked the time on her wristwatch.

"Okay, I think we're good."

"I thought we were going to wait an hour or so?" Lilian said. She didn't like it when plans changed. That was the whole point of having a plan – so you wouldn't rush into things that hadn't been thought through.

"We'll be fine," Serena insisted. "Even if somebody sees us, let's just say we're going outside to look at the stars as part of a science project or something."

Marian didn't seem convinced, but Lilian was fast discovering that nobody really argued with Serena. Unless she wanted your favourite seashell of course.

They tiptoed to the door. Serena opened it and glanced outside.

"It's clear, come on."

As quietly as they could, they crept along the corridor and down the stairs. To Lilian, their footsteps sounded like a herd of rampaging elephants, and every squeak, creak and crack made her wince. They heard laughter coming from a dorm room and all froze, but nobody appeared and so they continued on their way. It wasn't long before they reached the main door. Serena gave it a tug, but it was locked.

"Just the bolt," she whispered. "Hang on."

She slid it back, before opening the door, which groaned as if woken from a nice, comfortable snooze.

Then they were outside, thin wreaths of mist drifting over the grounds to meet them. Quickly, they dashed towards the lake, crouched over like thieves making their escape from a jewel heist. Lilian glanced back. They were already invisible to anyone that might happen to look out of the window. It gave her confidence. They would be back and safe in their beds before anyone knew they were gone.

Lilian knew the boat was still on the shoreline, but it was harder to find in the dark. Things looked different at night. Tall reeds swished in the wind. Cold water lapped at the edges of the shore. An owl hooted from somewhere in the woods. It was all so quiet out here. Finally, Lilian spotted the boat and ushered the girls towards it. It was small and light, and easy to push into the water.

"At last, shipmates," Serena said in her best pirate voice. "We have us a seafaring vessel, aaargh!"

"I'll row," Lilian said. "I've done it a few times when I was on holiday with my parents. There was a lake we used to go on and my dad showed me. It's pretty easy."

She waited until everyone was settled and seated, then

got in and grasped the oars. In her mind she heard her dad's voice.

You don't go out on the water without a life jacket, Lilian.

She knew he was right, but the island was only about twenty or thirty feet away. The lake was calm. The water didn't look deep, and when she stuck an oar in, it only came up halfway. You could stand up in it and still have your head above water. They would be fine.

"Stay seated, everyone, until we get across," she said.

"Aye, aye, captain," Serena replied with a salute.

Mist rose from the lake. The only sound was the splish-splash of the oars. In daytime, this would have been a pleasant outing. At night, it felt forbidden and dangerous. Lilian focused on keeping the strokes slow and even. And as she suspected, in just a few minutes they felt the boat crunch as it hit the opposite shore. The girls leaped out and pulled the boat up a couple of feet. There was a rope attached to the stern and Lilian stuck a heavy rock on top of it to keep the boat in place.

They turned on their torches and made their way through the reeds. Bats swooped above their heads.

"Hello, friends," Marian sighed.

Then they found a path. It wound around and around, like a spiral, so it felt as if they were walking in circles, but it wasn't long at all before the mausoleum came into view. Lilian flashed her torch across the exterior of the mausoleum. Smooth grey stone. The eye-catching dome on top. There were no weeping angels or winged cherubs. Lilian had been expecting something more ornate, but from the outside it was very plain.

"Feels like we're in a horror film, don't you think?" Marian said.

Nobody laughed.

"Look, the entrance is around here," Angela said. They were the first words she'd spoken since they'd left the school. Lilian felt proud to see her leading the way with no apparent trace of her usual nervousness.

Two stone columns flanked the entrance, but the doors themselves were wooden, with flaking blue paint. More like the entrance to someone's garden shed than the resting place of an aristocratic family. A heavy chain looped through the door handles and ended in a padlock. Why had she assumed it wouldn't be locked? It was so stupid. And now they'd come all this way for nothing.

"It's rusty," Lilian said, examining the lock. "Maybe we could lever it open?"

"With what, a packet of biscuits and an umbrella?" Serena said.

Reluctantly, Lilian let the padlock drop.

"Not really going to learn anything if we can't get inside," Marian said.

"Let me have another look," Lilian said. "In case we missed something."

She wandered around the mausoleum's exterior, pausing occasionally to press her hands against the walls, as if they might suddenly slide apart and reveal a secret entrance. She peered through cracks in the stonework but couldn't see anything except an old tangle of cobwebs. It was an impenetrable fortress. Lilian was so sure that there was something about Isobel's death to be discovered here. Sighing, she made her way back to join the others.

The mist had grown thicker and for a moment, Lilian thought she saw four figures waiting for her instead of three. Heart thudding, she peered through the foggy night, before realizing that the fourth figure was just a bush.

"Find anything?" Marian asked.

"Nope," Lilian said. "Not unless we can break that padlock."

"I'm going to take a picture of the mausoleum," Marian said. "For my personal collection."

"You goths really are odd," Serena muttered.

The girls watched as Marian held the camera up,

before snapping a picture. It slid out of the bottom a few seconds later and she placed it in her pocket.

Lilian was suddenly distracted by Angela, who'd gone as pale as the mists that swirled at their ankles. She was staring at the mausoleum doors, her face crunched up in a horrified frown. Slowly, she raised a finger and pointed at the door.

"L...look..." she stammered.

Lilian turned back to the mausoleum. At first, she couldn't decipher what she was supposed to be looking at. But then she saw it.

One of the door handles was slowly turning.

"Is it...moving?" Marian said.

"No...that's not...right," Serena gasped.

The movement was slow and deliberate, like watching the second hand on a clock. Lilian took a step back, feeling a strange, almost painful knot of fear in her stomach.

A second later, there was a soft creak and the door rattled slightly in its frame, as if someone had pushed their weight against it. Dust trickled down from the padlock. Lilian was frozen with fear, making it impossible to think clearly. What could possibly be pushing against the locked door from *inside*. It was Marian's voice that broke her brain freeze.

"Run!" she cried. "Quick, before the padlock breaks!"

It was one of those commands that didn't need to be debated or thought about. The girls fled as one, crunching through the reeds in their panic to find the boat and escape. Yet in their haste to get away, with the mists thicker than ever, and the tall reeds obscuring their view, they quickly lost their bearings.

"I think the boat's this way," Serena said.

"Are you sure?" Marian gasped. "I thought it was the other way."

"Don't worry," Lilian said. "It's only a small island, we'll find it."

Just then, Angela held up one pale hand and shushed them into silence.

"Listen," she whispered. "Something's out there."

They held their breath, exchanging wide-eyed glances. A second later, they heard it. A low rustling in the reeds. They stared in the direction the sound was coming from. The tops quivered as something moved slowly and carefully through them.

Without waiting, the four girls sprinted along the shore, not caring if they were heading in the right direction, as long as they were getting further away from whatever was behind them. They were running so fast they almost fell into the boat.

"Quick, get in, everyone," Lilian said, pushing it off the shore and into the water, hearing a cracking and snapping from behind them, as something forced its way through the vegetation.

The sides of the boat had got wet on the trip across, the old wood greasy and damp. Lilian could see it coming. Angela slipped as she climbed in, her flailing arms clutching at thin air. Serena made a desperate attempt to grab her, but it was too late. Angela fell sideways into the water with a strangled cry and a loud splash.

About to leap in after her, Lilian heard a crunch of gravel from the shore.

A figure stood, silhouetted in the mist.

Then it began running towards them.

Chapter 12

The figure leaped into the water with a splash and began wading towards their boat as it drifted slowly away from the shore. Marian gasped. Lilian was frozen. Angela flailed helplessly in the water. The figure paused for a second, then lunged towards Angela and grabbed her by the arms.

As Lilian reached for the oar, intending to strike them with it, the figure yanked Angela up from the shallow water. Serena's torch flashed into their pale face.

"Mr Bullen!" Lilian cried.

It was the history teacher, his soaked black clothes clinging to his wiry frame, so he looked like some kind of strange prehistoric bird that lived in the lake.

There was a huge sigh of relief all round.

"Give me a hand, would you?" he said, helping the equally bedraggled Angela towards the boat.

The girls reached out towards Mr Bullen as he gently lifted Angela in. She was shaking, the freezing water having numbed her limbs. Her glasses had slipped down her nose and her hair was plastered across one side of her face.

"Do you have anything dry to wrap her in?" Mr Bullen asked.

"Yes, sir," Marian said, delving into her backpack for a spare jumper, which they hurriedly pulled over Angela's head.

Mr Bullen stood in the lake, hands on his hips, the water up to his thighs.

"Now, girls, I shall come with you until you're safely back across. I won't ask what on earth you were doing over here. That can wait until tomorrow. Hurry, please, before she catches her death of cold."

Serena sniffed and glanced over the water as if this was a minor inconvenience. Marian flushed and bowed her head. For the moment, Lilian had forgotten all about the island and its mysteries. Now all she could think of was what might happen to them. Mr Bullen climbed in and held onto the stern of the boat, while Lilian did her best to row them smoothly back across.

They reached the opposite shore without incident and all helped Angela off the boat. Despite her insistence that she was fine, in the torchlight Angela's skin had a sickly blue pallor, and Lilian couldn't help but feel a deep wave of shame at having brought her out on a such a reckless expedition.

"Go inside and get her warmed up, quickly now," Mr Bullen said. "I shall be up to check on her shortly."

Strangely, instead of following them, he got in the boat again and began rowing back towards the island. In no time at all, the mists swallowed him up.

There were no jokes or smart comments now. The girls hurried back up to the school in silence, each one lost in their own thoughts, Lilian's being mostly about what on earth could have been making the door handle move from inside a locked mausoleum – could it have been Mr Bullen?

Lilian half expected to be greeted by an angry Ms Strange, but they entered the school the same way they had left it, along empty, silent corridors until they were back in their dormitory. They fetched towels and helped Angela dry off and get out of her wet clothes, before bundling her up in bed. They then quickly got into their own beds.

A short time afterwards, Mrs Benson, the nurse, popped her head around the door.

"Mr Bullen asked me to come and check on Angela," she explained.

The older lady walked in and sat on Angela's bed, checking her pulse and taking her temperature, before finally giving her something to swallow with a sip of water.

"It'll help you sleep, dear," Mrs Benson said to Angela. "I don't know what you all thought you were doing, going out on that lake at night, but I shall report back to Mr Bullen that there seems to be no harm done. I'd like you to come and see me in the morning though, Angela, okay?"

Angela nodded, before Mrs Benson wished them all goodnight.

After she'd left, the girls were silent for a few moments before Serena spoke.

"Do you think it was Mr Bullen then?" Serena said. "Inside the mausoleum?"

"I was thinking the same thing," Lilian said. "He seemed to arrive very quickly after Angela fell and it would explain why we saw the handle moving."

"But how could he padlock an old tomb from the inside?" Marian said. "It doesn't make sense."

"It makes as much sense as ghosts," Serena said. "You've said it yourself, he's a weird sort, maybe he was doing some of his historical research?"

Lilian could see them both up on their elbows, their shadowy outlines facing in her direction.

"That does seem plausible," Lilian said quietly.

"Well, hang on," Marian said. "You might want to look at this first."

She climbed out of her bed and came and sat on Lilian's, before holding out the photograph she'd taken on the island. Lilian reached for her torch and flicked it on. Serena and Angela climbed out of bed, too, and came over to take a look for themselves.

It showed the front of the mausoleum, looking stark and strange.

But in the foreground, there was a strange smudge on the photograph.

It might have been a bank of fog.

But it did look very much like the shadowy outline of a person.

After examining the photograph, the girls had returned to their beds without coming to an agreement as to what it had captured. The image flashed in Lilian's mind as she tried to fall asleep. Sometimes, when she'd looked at the photograph, it appeared to be just a bank of fog. But then she would look again and see the clear outline of a person – what looked like a young girl. Could it be the ghost of Isobel Boulogne? Was that who she'd seen in the woods, too? Perhaps it was Cold Mary? They still didn't know who had tried to draw Angela towards the lake either.

Lilian reached over to her bedside table where she kept the necklace that Mr Bullen had returned to her. Running her fingers over its silver links, she wondered if Isobel had ever seen it with her own eyes. It was a strange sensation to think that both she and a girl who had been dead for almost one hundred and fifty years might have touched the same thing. She lifted it over her head. She'd never worn it before and wondered what it felt like. It was surprisingly light.

Lilian laid her head back down on the pillow. What a day. And now that all the adrenalin had worn off, she dreaded the thought of waking up tomorrow and being in trouble again. Once Mr Bullen told Ms Strange what had happened, then it would be curtains. What if she was expelled? Lilian could just imagine how her parents would feel. They'd probably never speak to her again. But thinking about her parents reminded her of something her mum had told her once – that there was no point worrying about things you couldn't do anything about, as it would only stress you out. But it was easier said than done. Sighing, she closed her eyes and tried to clear her mind. She would worry about tomorrow…tomorrow.

Lying there in the darkness, Lilian listened to the wind rustling through the treetops. No wonder it was so cold in here. There were draughts coming from everywhere. Slowly, she felt her thoughts slow as sleepiness burrowed in beside her. She wondered what Susan and her parents were doing back at home. Susan would probably be asleep, cuddled up with her stuffed monkey which she was too old for. Her parents would be watching TV downstairs. She missed the sound of the television at night. It had always been comforting, knowing that her parents were close by. Though at least she wasn't alone in here. She dreaded to think what it would be like here without her new friends sleeping alongside her…

Lilian woke with a start.

It had felt like cold fingers had reached out and touched her neck in her sleep. For a second, she glimpsed something white and pale above her, but it was gone before her eyes could focus properly. A breath caught in her throat so fast that it hurt. Her heart thudded in her chest. She raised herself up and looked around the dormitory. Maybe it had been Angela, coming to share her bed again. But the other three girls were in their beds, the rise and fall of their blankets like waves on a midnight sea.

Lilian listened for a while. Outside, the wind had picked up, sounding more like an angry roar than a gentle hiss. There was a cold whisper on her cheek. Turning, she saw the door was slightly ajar. She remembered the nurse, Mrs Benson, closing it firmly behind her. And in all the excitement of the previous night, they'd forgotten to put their makeshift alarm system in place.

Climbing out of bed, Lilian stared wild-eyed around the room. The hatch above Angela's bed was still closed. Her fingers reached up and touched the necklace. Then she had a horrible realization. The thing she'd seen, the white moon-like shape that had hovered into view for a moment as she woke.

It had been a face.

The face of someone leaning over to look at her as she slept.

Pushing her feet into her slippers, she crept to the door. Pulling it open, she peered down the corridor, but it was silent and empty. She'd half-expected to see the back of someone as they ran away.

A hand gripped her shoulder.

Startled, she wheeled around.

"Whoa, easy tiger," Serena said.

"Oh, sorry," Lilian said. "You made me jump."

"I could see, you leaped about a foot in the air. What's got into you then?"

Lilian took one peek into the corridor, before pushing the door shut.

"Come here and I'll tell you," she said, beckoning Serena towards her bed.

Once they were settled, Lilian told Serena what had just happened.

"A nightmare, surely?" Serena said, though Lilian could plainly see the uneasy expression on her face.

"Don't think so," Lilian said, shaking her head. "I wish it was."

"I mean, what else could it have been – a ghost?" Serena asked.

"Maybe," Lilian said. "Because the reason I woke up was because I felt someone touch my neck."

"Ugh," Serena said. "Why would a ghost do that?"

Lilian reached inside her pyjamas and pulled out the necklace she was wearing.

"Because I think they were after this."

Chapter 13

After this unsettling incident, thankfully the day began to get better. Angela returned from Mrs Benson with a clean bill of health. And Serena had bumped into Mr Bullen, who told her that he wasn't going to mention anything to Ms Strange about their late-night adventure.

"He said he blamed himself," Serena said, as they picked at their lunch in the canteen. "He said that it was him that showed us the portrait of Isobel Boulogne in the first place and it made us overly curious."

"That's sort of true though," Marian said, pushing away a greasy chop with a look of disdain.

"He probably didn't expect us to immediately set sail for her family mausoleum," Angela said, which earned her a snort from Serena.

"I think that's very honourable of him," Lilian said. "I dread to think what would have happened if Ms Strange had found out."

"I'd give anything for my nani's home-made rogan josh right now," Serena said, pushing away her shepherd's pie. "Anyway, Lilian, did you tell the gang about your creepy visitor last night?"

Lilian laid down her fork and sighed. She'd been hoping Serena wouldn't mention it, particularly when she saw Angela's face pale. Marian raised her eyebrows and looked hurt.

"Why didn't you say anything?" she said.

"I was going to," Lilian said. "But after a while it began to feel a bit stupid, as though I might have imagined it."

"What exactly do you think you *imagined*?" Angela said, pushing her glasses back and fixing Lilian with a very pointed look.

Taking a deep breath, Lilian recounted what had happened. The sense of someone touching her neck. The face that loomed over her for a split second. The feeling that it had something to do with her wearing the mysterious C necklace.

"And so I'm going to take it back to Mr Bullen," Lilian said. "I don't think it should be worn by any of us. I was going to have to return it at some point anyway."

"Better *sooner than later*," Marian said. "You saw that girl in the woods, too, remember? You said it reminded you of Isobel Boulogne in the portrait. And the girl who tried to steal Angela away. Do you not think something could be after us?"

Nobody answered. Lilian glanced at Angela, who pretended to be inspecting a soggy broccoli stem. A sense of dread hung in the air. Lilian's body felt stiff and cold.

"Well, even if you lot are too scared to admit it, I'm not," Marian huffed. "We need to stick together like we said. Nobody should go anywhere in the school without at least one other roomie with them."

"I'm taking the necklace back to Mr Bullen after dinner," Lilian said. "I don't want it in the dormitory. Anyone fancy coming with me?"

"Yes," Serena said, immediately. "We'll all come."

And so, after dinner was done, Lilian retrieved the necklace from her bedside drawer and, together, they set off for Mr Bullen's office. The school was always quieter after dinner. The day girls had gone and the boarders mostly retreated to their dorms where it was comfier, warmer and there was a steady supply of biscuits. Sarah Shoesmith and Sally Baldwin were chatting in the doorway of their dormitory. They stopped and whispered as the girls approached.

"Where are you lot off to?" Sarah said. "You're not supposed to leave your dorm room in the evening."

"Official business," Serena said. "Which means, mind yours."

"Oh, that must mean you're going swimming in the lake again," Sally said with a snigger. "The Midnight Creepers strike again!"

Word had obviously got out.

"Well, we might be *creepers* but it's better than being just *creeps*," Serena snarled, causing Sally to quickly shut the door.

"How did they know about that?" Serena muttered.

"I might have mentioned it to Julie Atherton," Angela said. "We were waiting outside Mrs Benson's room together this morning and she asked me why I was there."

"I really need to teach you more about how this place works," Serena said. "For one, there is *never* such a thing as a private conversation. You could have just as easily gone up to the roof and shouted it through a megaphone."

They descended into the basement, the lamps on the

walls growing dimmer. There was nobody to be seen. A light shone out from Mr Bullen's office into the corridor, and as they approached, Lilian noticed that the door was open a fraction.

She reached out and knocked, which pushed the door open a little more. The office appeared to be empty.

"He's not here," Serena said. "Leave the necklace and let's get back to our dorm."

"Just a minute," Lilian said. She called out. "Hello, Mr Bullen, are you there?"

There was no reply. Lilian pushed the door open a little further.

"Mr Bullen?"

Although a fire crackled in the grate, the office was empty. A book lay open on the desk. A mug next to it was full of steaming tea. It looked like he'd just been here. Then Lilian noticed the gap in the bookcase. The one she'd seen on a previous visit.

"Look," she whispered, beckoning the others to follow. "There's the secret entrance I told you about."

"We should go," Angela said.

"Hang on one sec," Serena said. "Did you not hear Lilian say *secret entrance*?"

"We did knock," Lilian said. "Let's just have a quick

peek." She drew the necklace out of her pocket and held it up. "Besides, we have an excuse as to why we're in here."

As a group, they shuffled forward. Lilian could feel Angela's hand, resting lightly on her shoulder. Lilian reached out and gently pulled at the bookcase. It swung open with a loud creak. Inside, she could see a flickering lamp on the wall.

It was a tunnel.

The walls were brick, and appeared to gleam, as if they were damp.

"I don't believe it," Marian gasped. "Where does it lead?"

"Only one way to find out," Serena said.

Lilian led them in. The tunnel was narrow so they had to drop into single file, yet they'd barely all got inside before Lilian saw a flight of steps leading down.

But down where? Weren't they already on the lowest level?

"Mr Bullen?" Lilian called, hearing the tremor in her voice.

The only response was silence.

She glanced behind her.

"There are steps leading down," she said. Lilian knew

that the sensible thing would be to turn back and settle down in the dormitory with a biscuit and a book. But then Serena gave her a nudge in the small of her back, which was all the encouragement she needed.

"Keep going," Serena said. "We might not get another chance to see this."

The rough-hewn steps sloped in the middle. They appeared very old. One step at a time, nerves on edge, they descended.

And found themselves in another tunnel.

It was dimly lit and very cold. Lilian could see every breath she took coming out in a huge grey fog. Here the walls were also made of old brick, parts of which had been covered with plaster. Lilian had an idea where this was leading but she kept her suspicions to herself for now. She didn't want to scare anyone off.

This part of the tunnel had electric lights. Despite this modern touch, there was still an undeniable sense of being in a very old place. Water dripped down from the ceiling, leaving brown puddles on the floor. The lights buzzed, flickering on and off as if they weren't quite getting enough power. The tunnel widened enough so they could now walk abreast of each other.

They began at a snail's pace, exchanging nervous

glances while trying not to talk. Somehow, they all understood that being as quiet as possible was a good idea. The tunnel appeared to be leading them straight underneath the grounds. Soon, the water dripping from overhead increased. In places, it was more like a stream of water than a few drips. Lilian's feet splashed in puddles that smelled of dank weeds and mud.

"We're not...underneath the lake, are we?" Marian asked, breaking the silence.

"I think so," Lilian said with a gulp.

Above them swirled thousands of gallons of dark water and Lilian couldn't help but imagine the roof of the tunnel suddenly giving way. They would be drowned in an instant. This disturbing mental image forced her to move faster and, soon, the tunnel rose and it became dryer, which was a relief to all.

Finally, Lilian saw an iron ladder leading up.

She reached the bottom and listened, but all she could hear was dripping water, like the second hand on a hundred clocks.

"What should we do now?" Marian asked, peering up.

"Go up, I suppose," Lilian said. "We have to see where it leads."

Grasping the cold, damp rungs, she began to climb

until she reached what looked like a trapdoor.

She pushed at it with one hand but it didn't budge. Making sure she was secure on the ladder, she raised both hands up and pushed with all her strength. This time it creaked open.

Lilian felt something brush against her face. She hastily swatted at it. *Just a cobweb*, she reassured her thumping heart. She climbed up through the opening and waited for her eyes to become accustomed to the gloom. She was standing on a flagstone floor in a dimly lit chamber. A lamp hung on the wall, flickering feebly. Around her, Lilian could discern the outlines of individual tombs, as if she was surrounded by a sleeping family made of white stone. The tombs were stacked on levels, two on ground level, two above that and then two more up high, close to the ceiling. For a moment, Lilian's emotions hovered between excitement and terror. Because now she knew that she was standing inside the ancestral tomb of the Boulogne family, where they'd been laid to rest for hundreds of years.

Raising one hand in front of her face, she stared at it, willing it to stop trembling. She could leave right now, but if she did, then she might never know if this mausoleum held any secrets, and so she forced herself to stay still.

Thick clusters of cobwebs congregated in the upper corners of the tomb's ceiling. The air smelled thick and stale, but not altogether unpleasant – the aroma of stillness and age. But as Lilian turned to call the others up, she noticed something unusual.

Footprints.

Clearly visible in the dust, which had kept a record of someone passing through, almost like a signature. As far as Lilian knew, even if ghosts existed, they didn't leave footprints. Was this where Mr Bullen went? And why did his office have a secret passage that led here? Her nerves felt like shards of glass and she kneeled by the trapdoor, eager to reassure herself that her friends were still behind her.

"What's going on up there?" Serena hissed from below.

"The ladder leads up into the mausoleum," Lilian whispered. "There are tombs and everything. Only, I think Mr Bullen's somewhere in here, too."

"Hold on, I'm coming up."

Serena pushed herself up on the ladder and took it all in with a quick glance.

"Wow," she said, before calling back down. "Marian, I think I've found your new home."

Serena climbed up and they waited for Angela and then Marian to join them.

"I've never been in a mausoleum before," Angela said, her glasses steamed up from the cold.

"This is amazing," Marian whispered, giving the place a wide-eyed stare. "Wow, look at all the graves."

"Let's look around," Lilian said. "Isobel Boulogne's tomb must be here somewhere. There might be something on it that can tell us how she died."

Turning her attention to the tombs themselves, the graves within a grave, she began to take a closer look, conscious that they should be as quick as possible. She didn't want to get caught and they hadn't even begun exploring the first chamber. A stone archway led through to more chambers, which meant more tombs to explore. Bending down, Lilian read the one closest to her.

Edward Boulogne, 1723–1767.

On top of it was the carved figure of a man, though it had crumbled away in parts and Lilian couldn't really make out his face. Opposite it was another similar-sized tomb. This one was in better condition and had a carving of a lady on top, hands folded, eyes closed. She looked very peaceful, as if she'd just fallen asleep. On this one was written:

Antoinette Boulogne, 1732–1791.

The dates on this tomb were similar to the previous one. Was this Edward's wife? Or sister? They must be Isobel's ancestors. There was no mention of how Edward or Antoinette had died, which was disappointing, but Lilian hadn't given up hope just yet. There were more tombs above these, but without a ladder they were too high up for Lilian to read. She hoped Isobel's wasn't up there.

Lilian walked on, aware that the other girls were following her closely in a very tight huddle. She could understand why. Cold moonlight shone in through small windows high up near the mausoleum's roof. Shadows sprang up out of the darkness, so it felt like there was always someone else creeping along beside them. Their footsteps scraped on the stone floor. Their breathing was light and quick.

The mausoleum appeared to be organized into four separate chambers, like a cross, each one with different members of the Boulogne family in it. Lilian walked to the centre and glanced along each passageway. There was no sign of anyone else in here. If Mr Bullen had come down here from his office, had he returned to the school another way? Was there another secret passage somewhere? She remembered his sudden appearance at the lake. What if there were tunnels everywhere? Maybe he had just left through the door and rowed back across?

The back of Lilian's neck was growing colder by the minute and she began to get the distinct and awful feeling that there *was* someone in here. Someone, perhaps, who wasn't warm and breathing. She couldn't explain exactly why. Just a sense of being observed. Of a presence silently watching them from a dark corner. She glanced at her watch. They needed to get a move on. She was beginning to feel scared.

Right on cue, Angela whispered in the dark. "Can we go now?"

"I'm ready, too," Serena said. "Feels like we shouldn't be in here."

"I never thought I'd say this," Marian added. "But even I think we should get going."

"Just one minute, I promise I'll be quick," Lilian said.

Steeling herself, she stared down the passageways, trying to decide which one to explore.

Then she saw something which made her eyes widen in the half-light.

All the other tombs seemed to follow a pattern. A carved outline lying on top of a simple stone sarcophagus. A representation of whoever lay inside. This one was different. The carving on this tomb showed someone standing up. It also had its own large alcove with nothing else beside it or above it. With the others following, Lilian tiptoed towards it, as if not wanting to wake anything that might be sleeping.

The carving was of two young girls, their limbs entwined so it was impossible to see which arms and legs belonged to which girl. One girl looked to the right. She had a calm, serene expression, as if she'd been happy in life. The other girl looked to the left and appeared sad, the eyes sunken and downcast, the mouth slightly parted as if caught at the moment of a sorrowful sigh. It was peculiar and unsettling. Below it, there was a name.

Isobel Boulogne, 1826–1838.

"I can't believe it," Lilian whispered. "We've found her."

She scrambled around, looking for any other writing – an explanation, a cause of death – anything. The tomb was thick with dust. But there had to be something.

"Why does it show two girls on the grave?" Angela said, peering up at the carving.

Marian had kneeled down and was wiping at the stone below Isobel's name.

"Because there's another name on the tomb," she said

quietly, pointing a finger at where she'd scraped away the dust.

Lilian glanced down. She could barely believe her eyes.

Catherine Boulogne, 1826–1837.

Lilian noticed the dates. Born in the same year. Either sisters that were very close in age or…

The word flashed into her mind.

"Twins," she whispered. "Isobel had a twin!"

"C for Catherine," Serena whispered.

A sound behind her made them start. The girls clutched at each other. Angela let out a small gasp.

A figure stood silhouetted in the gloom, eyes sparkling like dark jewels.

Instinctively, the girls took a backwards step.

Slowly, the figure raised a hand and pointed towards them.

Chapter 14

Lilian felt her body grow weak.

"W-who…are…" she gasped.

The figure flicked on a torch and shone it into their eyes.

"Good evening, girls. Out for another late-night stroll, I see," a voice said.

As Lilian squinted, the figure lowered the torch.

"Mr Bullen," Lilian gasped. "You nearly scared us to death again!"

At that moment, Lilian was too relieved to be afraid of the consequences of being caught in here. She was glad to see him.

"Pardon the intrusion," Mr Bullen said. "But I generally don't expect to find anyone else in here. Nobody alive that is. Particularly girls that have already been warned about venturing to forbidden places. Not only are you out alone and unsupervised, but you appear to be rifling through a private mausoleum like a gang of grave robbers."

"We're not here to steal anything," Lilian said, feeling a quick wash of fiery heat ripple through her cold body.

"No offence intended, Lilian," Mr Bullen said. "Though I *would* be curious to know why you all thought it appropriate to walk through a tunnel that can only be accessed from my office."

"We were looking for you, sir," Marian said, quickly. "We wanted to return the necklace but you weren't there."

"Thought you might have had an accident or something," Angela said, earning her an impressed look from Serena.

"And we didn't know the tunnel led here," Serena added.

"Well, I appreciate your concern, however…" Mr Bullen trailed off with a frown, before shining his torch around the mausoleum. Lilian saw him run his fingers around his neck.

"I'm not sure this is the best place for a chat," he said. "Let's get you back to school first."

He motioned for them to follow him. Lilian gave the

tomb of Isobel and Catherine Boulogne a final glance. Twin sisters. It couldn't be a coincidence that Mary Atkins and Lucy Groves had both been seen with a twin, too. And then there was the incident with Angela. Whatever the mystery was, it appeared to be creeping closer and closer. There *had* to be a connection. The frustrating thing was that Lilian couldn't quite see it yet.

It made her think about the portrait of Isobel and the skull girl she'd seen in Mr Bullen's office. Having two people in the painting made more sense now. They also knew how Mr Bullen had been able to get to the island and back without them knowing. While they were huffing and puffing away on a rowing boat, he'd been using the tunnel. What a perfect way to travel unseen. It *must* have been him inside the mausoleum that night, rattling the handle, which gave her a sense of relief. Though it still begged the question: why was he in there? And how did he manage to unlock a padlock from the inside?

Now, it appeared they were all going to pay a heavy price for her insatiable curiosity. And as Lilian followed Mr Bullen to the trapdoor that led back down into the tunnel, she wondered if this would be the last night she'd spend at Shadowhall Academy.

They descended into the tunnel and began walking,

in silence at first, though Lilian noticed that every few seconds, the teacher would cast a glance back over his shoulder, as if he'd heard something behind them.

"Quickly now, girls," Mr Bullen said. "No time to dawdle."

Lilian fell in beside him.

"There's a connection here, isn't there, sir?" Lilian said, quietly. "With the twins."

"What do you mean exactly?" Mr Bullen replied, shuffling along in his strange crab-like walk.

"Those girls who went missing. Mary Atkins. Lucy Groves. They were seen with girls who were identical to them, even though that was impossible. And now there's the two Boulogne girls in the mausoleum…and the painting…"

From behind them, they heard what sounded like an anguished moan. A cry of either despair – or anger. The girls stopped, turning to peer back up the tunnel.

"What was that?" Angela said, looking to Mr Bullen for reassurance.

"Just the wind, Angela," Mr Bullen replied, though Lilian was convinced that he'd grown even paler than usual. "It travels through this tunnel at quite a rate and makes some extraordinary sounds. But come on, let's step up the pace. We're nearly home."

They did as he asked. Despite her curiosity, Lilian was keen to get back into the school, where there would at least be light. And people.

A few minutes later, they were inside Mr Bullen's office, having almost run the last few feet. He closed the bookshelf firmly behind him.

"Well, I suppose the secret tunnel is no longer secret, is it?" Mr Bullen said. "Anyway, girls, it's getting late. May I propose we talk about this tomorrow? There are things you already know about this school, it seems. And there are things you are yet to discover. But now is the time to be safe and warm in your beds."

Lilian thought about what to say next. She liked Mr Bullen and felt she could trust him. And so she steeled herself.

"But, Mr Bullen, if there's danger here, we need to know right now, don't we? Angela left the school the other night with a girl who looked just like her and who told her that she needed to go down to the lake. Only, the girl who was with her disappeared."

"It's true," Angela said. "And I don't want to be another missing girl. I wouldn't be here right now if it wasn't for Lilian."

"Oh dear," Mr Bullen said quietly.

"And the necklace we found in the wall, it belonged to Isobel's sister, didn't it?" Lilian continued, sensing that her concerns were finally being heard. "C for Catherine. It's got to be hers. So please tell us – what's happening here? Why didn't you tell us Isobel had a twin?"

Mr Bullen cast a nervous glance back at the bookshelf, before pursing his lips and bowing his head. When he raised it again, he wore a grim expression.

"Very well, we'll talk."

He showed them to the chairs opposite his desk, before taking a seat himself. Leaning over, he flicked on the kettle that sat on the small table and placed five teabags into cups.

"I don't know about you, girls, but a hot cup of Darjeeling seems like a very good idea."

They waited for the kettle to boil in silence before Mr Bullen poured the water into the cups and added milk, then asked them each in turn if they took sugar or not. As before, this whole process seemed to drag on, with clinks of spoons, repeated stirs, and dangled teabags, but eventually, Mr Bullen handed them their tea and they all took a sip. A plate of custard creams was also passed around. At least his biscuits had improved, Lilian thought. While the girls munched and blew on their hot tea,

Mr Bullen leaned forward in his chair and sighed.

"I have a small confession to make. I admit to knowing a great deal about Shadowhall Academy that has nothing to do with my role here as teacher. My name, well, *Bullen*, is an anglicized version of a much older version. My original family name is Boulogne."

"You're related to the family that used to live here!" Lilian gasped, almost dropping her tea in her lap.

Mr Bullen nodded.

"Yes, a distant relative, not a direct descendant. But I did know about this place before I applied for the teaching post. I knew my ancestors had lived here, you see, so there was an added appeal. Once I was accepted, in my spare time I began to look through the archives and research the family history. I found it all very fascinating. I even stumbled across an old map which showed the location of this secret tunnel. I decided to move my office here so I could investigate it further, discovering in the process that it led to the Boulogne mausoleum."

"So that was you rattling the handle inside the mausoleum?" Serena asked. "The last time we were on the island?"

"Making sure it was locked, yes, so that no wandering students could get in. It was a good thing I checked, too.

The lock broke shortly after I tested it, hence why I was able to exit from the inside. However, it was during the course of this amateur research that I became aware of a dark legend that hangs over the Boulogne family, and as a result, it hangs over this school, their ancestral birthplace."

"It's something to do with Isobel and Catherine Boulogne," Lilian said. "I know it."

"Yes, you're right," Mr Bullen said, inclining his head towards her. "May I ask how you joined the dots?"

"It's the twins thing," Lilian said. "Not just what happened with the girls who disappeared, but it's everywhere in the school, too. I saw it on my first day – the gargoyle on the gate. Then the lions on the banisters. The snakes around your fireplace. The wolves on the tapestry in the dining hall. But it's only now making sense. This place, there's…two of everything, everywhere in this house. Once you see it, you can't not notice it."

"It's true," Marian said. "Double everything."

"Even double maths," Serena said with a half-hearted smile.

Mr Bullen steepled his fingers together.

"It is rather in plain sight, isn't it? A warning for those who see!"

Lilian shuffled in her seat.

"A warning?"

"This building, these grounds, they come with the curse of the Boulogne family. And you're right, it all begins – and ends I might say – with the twin girls, Isobel and Catherine. They lived back in the early 1800s. Their life was comfortable, happy. Their futures looked bright. But they weren't just twins, they were *identical*. And like many identical twins, they had almost a preternatural rapport."

"What does that mean?" Marian asked, hugging her tea to her chest. "That they were close?"

"More than that," Mr Bullen said. "According to the family journals I've read, they were like two halves of the same whole. They did everything together. Wore the same clothes. Liked the same things. Spoke in the same voice. Had the same mannerisms. They appeared to share an almost telepathic relationship, knowing what the other was going to say before they said it. It was said that often, one twin would begin a sentence, and then the other would finish it. But one day, Catherine disappeared. You can imagine how this affected her twin."

This tale was getting darker and more intriguing by the minute. Lilian forgot all about her tiredness and leaned forward, willing Mr Bullen to continue.

"She must have been very upset," Lilian said.

"Heartbroken," Angela added, with a soft sniff.

"Heartbroken indeed," Mr Bullen said, giving Angela a small nod. "It was as if Isobel's very soul had been ripped from her body. Catherine was never found, you see. Despite extensive searches of the grounds and beyond, she had gone. To this day, no one knows where. Perhaps if she *had* been found and there'd been a body, a funeral, Isobel may have had something to focus her grief on and things may have turned out differently."

Lilian knew there was more to this story than just a terrible tragedy.

"So, what happened after that?"

"Time passed. Isobel refused to talk. To anyone, not even her parents. She stayed in her room, surrounded by her sister's belongings. The family brought the country's best doctors to see her to try and find some way through this impenetrable wall of grief that she'd built, but one by one, they would shake their heads and concede that they could find no way to relieve her. Isobel became like a shadow. She would only move around the house at night. Her skin never saw the sun and she became deathly pale. One contemporary account I read stated that her eyes became so starved of daylight that they became unnaturally large and black, the pupils trying to compensate for the lack of natural light. Apparently, she would stand in dark corridors, whispering to herself. The servants eventually began to grow afraid of her midnight wanderings and refused to enter her room. Visitors stayed away. The house began to feel as if a great weight had been placed upon both it and its inhabitants."

Mr Bullen paused to take a sip of tea. The girls exchanged a nervous glance before Mr Bullen continued.

"Then, of course, the anniversary of Isobel's twin sister's disappearance came along. And after that, nothing was ever the same."

Chapter 15

Lilian heard a slow creak. Jumping up in her seat, she turned to see the door swing open a fraction, but there was nobody there. Mr Bullen got to his feet and closed it.

"It's always doing that," he said. "Like I say, the wind travels in strange directions down here in the basement. Now, I must warn you, girls, the story takes rather a dark turn at this point."

"We have to know," Lilian said.

"We're not afraid," Serena said, which earned her a questioning glance from Angela.

Mr Bullen smiled, which was possibly the first time Lilian had seen his face without a creased frown.

"I know you're not afraid," he said. "I don't know

many people your age that would go and investigate a mausoleum on their own at night. I don't know many people of any age in fact."

"There's nothing to be afraid of, when you think about it," Lilian said. "It's just a place where dead bodies are buried."

"Yes, quite," Mr Bullen said, looking down at his hands.

"So, what happened on the anniversary of Catherine's disappearance?" Marian asked.

Mr Bullen took a sip of tea and gulped it down rather loudly.

"The family were aware that this would be a very poignant date for Isobel. It was a poignant date for them all. They made every effort to stay close to Isobel, to show her that she was loved. But she was even more withdrawn than usual, refusing to move from her bedroom, her large, dark eyes fixated on something beyond the window. When the family awoke the next morning, Isobel's bed was empty and hadn't been slept in. They searched the house from top to bottom, but when no trace could be found, they extended the search to the grounds. That was when they found her."

"What happened?" Lilian said.

"She'd drowned. Her body was found by the shore of

the lake. It was returned to the house and the cause of death was confirmed at an inquest."

"That's awful," Angela whispered.

They lapsed into silence for a moment before Mr Bullen gave a nervous cough.

"But then, Isobel came back."

The back of Lilian's neck prickled with goosebumps.

"What do you mean, *came back*? She was dead, wasn't she?"

Mr Bullen sighed.

"Quite dead. But a year later, on the anniversary of her death, two years after Catherine's disappearance, Isobel was seen walking through the grounds by a servant. Of course, everybody assumed the servant had been mistaken. But shortly after, a local girl went missing. Nobody had seen anything suspicious, except for the girl's brother, who reported that he'd seen his sister with another girl."

Lilian held her breath. She knew what was coming.

"And the girl her brother saw?" she prompted.

"Her brother claimed that this girl had looked exactly like his sister – only his sister didn't have a twin. A year later, on the very same day, it happened again. Isobel was seen in the woods by a family member, her uncle. There could be no mistake this time, her uncle knew her as well as anyone. And shortly after, another girl went missing. And again, the only clue to her disappearance was that she was seen talking to a mysterious figure who bore an uncanny resemblance to her. She didn't have a twin either."

"Surely people were afraid?" Marian said.

"Indeed," Mr Bullen said. "That was why these stories quickly attracted attention. What would be the chances of two missing girls being seen with mysterious replicas of themselves? And these disappearances happened again. And again. And again."

Lilian was aghast.

"What about the other disappearances?" she said.

"The details have largely been lost it seems," Mr Bullen replied. "Simply short anecdotes that indicate their similarity to previous incidents. A missing child. An inexplicable double of them seen around the same time.

"The Boulogne family came to believe that Isobel's desire to be reunited with her twin sister extended beyond the grave. That she returns to search for a *new* twin. And so she takes on the exact appearance of her victims. We can read of similar accounts in folklore."

Lilian was open-mouthed with shock. It seemed too

preposterous to be true. And yet, it made sense of everything they'd been investigating. Mary Atkins, Lucy Groves – they must have been more victims of Isobel.

"So…when is the anniversary of Catherine's disappearance?" Lilian asked.

"The exact day was never recorded, but sometime in late October."

"And a girl disappears every anniversary?"

"No, in fact, after those first two, Isobel wasn't seen again for many years. The reason for her appearances remains something of a puzzle. There seems to be no rhyme or reason to them."

"It's late October now," Angela said with a quiver in her voice. "Lilian thinks she saw her in the woods. Someone who looked like me tried to lead me to the lake. I think Isobel has returned."

"Oh dear, oh dear," Mr Bullen said, his face ashen. "I always ascribed the story to old superstition. Bizarre explanations offered when no rational one could be found. Though I must admit, I have heard things in the mausoleum that were hard to explain. What sounded like whispers in the walls."

"So, what should we do?" Lilian said. "We can't just wait around for it to happen again."

"We must be extra vigilant," Mr Bullen replied. "I already like to walk the grounds at night, and well, you know of my research in the mausoleum. But from now on I shall spend my evenings patrolling the school and its grounds. As the saying goes, better safe than sorry."

Lilian looked at Mr Bullen with a fearful expression. If he was even the tiniest bit nervous, then she and the girls should be, too.

"It's late – I must bring our conversation to an end," Mr Bullen said, rising from his chair. "I'll walk with you up to your dormitory. You must be tired and possibly scared by what I've told you, but you needn't be. I'm here and I'm on guard now. If Isobel *has* decided to make an appearance, then together we shall thwart any nefarious plans she might have."

The girls followed him up to their dormitory. Lilian couldn't resist glancing into every shadowy corner. They heard footsteps running down the staircase and all of them tensed, even Mr Bullen. But it was just Vicki Atkinson, one of the senior girls, who gave them all a strange look as if sensing their nervousness. Once back at their dormitory, Mr Bullen smiled at each of them in turn.

"Well, I'll bid you all goodnight. We'll say no more of tonight's excursion. I have no wish to see any of you reprimanded, particularly seeing as we all appear to have been investigating the same rather dark subject. But perhaps you'll consider staying in for the next few evenings?"

Mr Bullen smiled again, and Lilian couldn't help but smile back.

"Yes, sir."

"Goodnight then."

"Goodnight, sir," they said.

Once they'd entered the dorm, barricaded the door, and got comfy in their beds, Lilian realized she'd forgotten to return the necklace. Now she knew it most likely belonged to Catherine, the long-lost twin, it was an unsettling feeling and she stuffed it right at the back of her bedside drawer before locking it.

Serena was the first to speak.

"Alright, gang, hands up who believes all that...about Isobel Boulogne?"

"I do," Marian said, raising a hand. "And I don't think we should leave this room until next summer."

Angela nibbled nervously on a biscuit, before slowly raising her hand, too.

"Mr Bullen is trying to reassure us," Lilian said, raising her hand as well. "But the facts speak for themselves.

Girls have gone missing here for hundreds of years. Cold Mary. Lucy Groves. The ones that Mr Bullen mentioned. All of them seen with someone who looked just like them. We need to be on our guard because we might be targets. Particularly after dark."

"But you saw Isobel during the day?" Marian said.

"Yes, but she didn't do anything except stare and laugh. And I was lost and feeling pretty helpless at the time. Maybe she's weaker during the day? Bad things are always more powerful at night."

"It gets dark early now," Angela said in a shaky voice.

"Then we'll be on our guard early," Lilian said.

They brushed their teeth in their room that night, using a water basin. None of them fancied the prospect of standing in a cold, dripping bathroom after everything they'd learned.

Lilian lay back on her bed and tried to clear her head. If Isobel had made a return, how could they stop her? And why had she come back now? Lilian believed that she'd seen Isobel in the woods, so did that make *her* the target? The thought was very unsettling. And yet it was Angela that had left in the middle of the night with a double. So, if Angela was the target, what was it about her in particular?

Also, Lilian remembered Mr Bullen mentioning something about *similar accounts in folklore*. So if there were other creatures like Isobel, then perhaps she could find some clues about how to deal with them? Tomorrow, she would go and visit Miss Coates again and see if she had any books on folklore where she might find some answers.

They'd decided that one of them would stay awake and keep watch. Marian was first, but Lilian was still wide awake by the time her turn came and she went to sit on Marian's bed.

"I haven't slept a wink," Lilian whispered. "I can't stop thinking about Isobel. You know, I think we need to keep a close eye on Angela. After what happened when she went out the other night, she might be the one who's in the most danger."

"Well, I'll certainly keep an eye out. I'll keep two eyes out." Marian leaned up out of bed and wrapped her arms around Lilian's shoulders. "I'm glad you decided to come to Shadowhall, Lilian."

Lilian returned her embrace.

"I'm not sure I am, Maz," Lilian said, with a grim smile. "But I'm glad I met you."

Then Lilian returned to her bed, arranged the pillows,

and spent the next few hours watching the door, jumping at every little creak.

After the drama of the previous evening, Lilian felt relieved to have a normal school day. Here in these lessons were things she knew to be facts. Questions had answers. There was right and wrong, with no grey murky areas in-between. Logic and science, instead of stories and myths. And yet it didn't quite ease her fears. Every time there was a lull in the class, or she was walking between lessons, Lilian's thoughts kept returning to what might or might not be lurking in the dark corners of Shadowhall Academy. It felt doubly strange to sit and see all the relaxed faces of those around her compared to the worried faces of her dorm mates.

As the day wore on, Lilian knew that soon the sun would set. The school would grow quieter and colder. The shadows would lengthen. The mists would gather. The birds would stop singing. The day girls would go home, leaving the school feeling emptier. The moon would paint the grounds with its eerie silver light. And perhaps, just perhaps, things that shouldn't really exist would begin to stir.

If such things were real, Lilian wanted more information about what they might be dealing with. And answers to questions were generally found in books. That was why, when lessons finished for the day, and Lilian had an hour before supper, she headed to the library. She told the other girls not to worry because Miss Coates would be there. She would feel safe with the friendly librarian by her side and anyway, it was still daylight.

Usually, there would always be at least one other girl in the library. But today was different. As Lilian pushed the door open, she had the immediate sense that it was empty. It wasn't just the silence that told her she was there alone. Empty places always felt *empty* – the lack of bodies and warmth and breathing leaving a cold vacuum in their wake.

"Miss Coates?" she called. "Are you in here?"

There was no reply. Lilian knew that she should immediately turn around and come back later. And yet, she couldn't bring herself to leave without having a quick look at the books. It would only take a few minutes.

Shivering, she took a deep breath and quickly began her search. Lilian remembered that Miss Coates had a specific section for paranormal books. And so that's where her search began.

There were lots of promising titles. Books about folklore and legends that might contain some answers. She selected a few and took them to the back, where there was a small desk that overlooked the grounds. Glancing out of the window, she could see mists beginning to creep towards the house. Even though it was still late afternoon, the horizon was already a dark smudge of purple, like a bruised apple. It would be dark very soon. Shivering, she wrapped her scarf a little tighter around her neck.

As she was studying a book about Irish folklore, she heard the library door creak open. She raised her nose out of her book and glanced towards the doorway. She could see someone moving between the aisles, but it was just another bookworm by the looks of it and she returned to her reading. At least she wasn't alone now. Occasionally she would hear a soft rustling as whoever it was moved between the shelves.

Meanwhile, her research was coming along. Lilian had found a few mentions of something called a *fetch* in Irish folklore. It seemed they were, like Isobel, always the exact doubles of people. The origin of the name was said by some to refer to the fact that the creature would literally "fetch" souls and take them off to the underworld.

There were unsettling accounts too, including one where a lady had taken tea with an older woman, only to discover upon her return that the woman had already died, and she'd been eating cake with the older woman's *fetch*. Unfortunately, there was no information on how to defeat them, although all the stories were connected to unhappy events.

Unhappy.

The word lingered in Lilian's mind, unwilling to move on, as if wanting her to think some more about it.

Mary Atkins had been unhappy. Miss Coates had mentioned something about her being upset that her parents were divorcing. Lucy Groves was unhappy, too. Her parents had died of typhoid and she was forced to become a servant. Lilian's eyes widened. Was Isobel drawn to girls who were sad? It would make sense. Because Isobel was unhappy, too. She'd lost her twin, without ever knowing what had happened. Maybe, Isobel wanted to be with girls just like her? Those who couldn't escape their sadness?

Lilian saw movement out of the corner of her eye and glanced towards the shelves. A figure ducked quickly into one of the aisles. Lilian stood up, trying to see where the person had gone. The sun had set by now and, outside, the mists had claimed the night for their own. They swirled outside the windows like a swarm of ghosts seeking shelter for the night. Gulping, Lilian decided that this was a good time to stop and gathered her books. She didn't want to be in the library any longer. Something didn't feel right. As she pushed the books back into their correct spots, she heard movement on the other side of the shelf. Whoever she was sharing the library with was now standing directly opposite her.

"Hello?" Lilian said softly, feeling her heart quicken its pace.

In return, she heard what sounded like laughter, a dark little chuckle that set Lilian's heart pounding even faster. It sounded very much like a laugh she'd heard before.

Slowly, she reached forward and pulled out the book nearest to her. The one at eye level. As it came away, Lilian peered through the gap.

A single, huge black eye stared back.

Lilian yanked another book out and found herself looking at something that made her whole body grow stiff with fear.

A grinning face.

A face that she knew all too well.

Chapter 16

It was Angela.

Only…it wasn't.

This creepy, twisted version of Angela had skin so pale and translucent it looked like parchment paper. Her eyes were unnaturally large and entirely black, as if someone had replaced the real ones with shining black pebbles. The skin was drawn tight over the face, so Lilian could see the taut bones beneath.

Crying out, Lilian recoiled, the books in her hand thudding to the floor. The figure behind the shelf darted away. The door creaked open and the Angela-not-Angela fled down the corridor. Lilian waited for a moment. Her body had momentarily forgotten how to breathe. When her breaths finally returned, they came in a panicked stampede. Slowly, Lilian focused until they returned to something like normal.

Even the tiniest doubt she'd had about what Mr Bullen told her immediately disappeared. The story *was* true. She had just met Isobel Boulogne. She had seen the *fetch*, the supernatural double that heralded death. It was as if Angela had been replicated by something much older, had lost the sparkle behind her eyes, replaced by a dark cunning that even now made Lilian's skin ripple with unease.

Angela.

Lilian had to get back. This had been her warning. Confirmation that Isobel Boulogne wanted her quiet, nervous and unhappy friend to be her new twin. It felt like Isobel had been taunting her.

This is who I'm going to take and there's nothing you can do about it.

Lilian ran as fast as she could along the corridors, ignoring the stares of other girls as she darted past like a dog chasing a rabbit. She climbed up the stairs, her breaths coming in ragged gasps, until she reached the dormitory and barged the door open.

Serena glanced up at her. She was lying on her stomach on her bed, reading. When she saw Lilian's face, the book dropped onto the sheets.

"Um…ahoy there…what's the matter?"

"It's her, she's…here," Lilian gasped. "I saw her in the l-library. Isobel Boulogne!"

Serena looked as horrified as Lilian felt.

"What! Are you sure?"

"Quite sure," Lilian said. "She looked exactly like Angela. Well, except that all the life was gone from her. And the eyes, all huge and black, just like in her portrait. It was her alright. It's not something you forget."

"That's horrible!" Serena said.

Lilian had never seen Serena look quite so frightened before. Usually she had a confident answer for everything.

"And I worked out why Isobel wants Angela, too," Lilian continued.

"You did?" Serena said.

"Because Angela's unhappy, like Isobel. All the girls she takes are the same. She's drawn to sadness because she understands it. Where is Angela? We have to find her!"

"She just went to the loo," Serena said. "But Angela's not sad."

Lilian frowned. She was sure her theory was correct.

"Are you sure?"

"Of course. We've been chatting a lot. She loves it here. Says her dad was always moving her from school to school and she had never had a chance to make friends. Says she hasn't been this happy in years. If anyone's sad, it's Marian."

"What?" Lilian said.

"Yes," Serena said. "Her mum's ill and they're waiting for test results to come back but it looks pretty serious. She told me she can't sleep at night for worrying."

Lilian had no idea what to say. She was so sure that Angela was the target. Hadn't Isobel Boulogne indicated as much? And to think that she had no idea about how Marian was feeling made her feel ashamed. They were supposed to be friends. Why hadn't she noticed? She couldn't remember ever stopping to ask Marian how she was. Marian would always ask her. Right now, she felt like a terrible friend. But if it was Marian who was in danger, then Lilian still had a chance to prove she could be counted on.

"Then we have to find Marian right now!" Lilian cried.

The door opened behind them, and Angela walked in.

"What's the matter?" Angela said. "Why are you both staring at me?"

"Do you know where Maz is?" Lilian said, feeling a dead weight in her stomach that had nothing to do with hunger.

"I thought she went to find you in the library?"

"I was just there and I didn't see her," Lilian said. "We need to go and find her, right now."

They dashed downstairs and into the dining hall. It seemed the most likely place to start their search seeing as it was supper time. The hum of happy conversation seemed strangely out of place. As they scanned the crowd, Lilian knew instantly that Marian wasn't there. Grabbing Serena and Angela, she ran out, aware that Mr Bullen jumped to his feet and cast an anxious glance in their direction. But she didn't have time for explanations.

"Let's check the dorm room one more time. Maybe we missed her and she's gone back up?" Lilian said, feeling her legs protest as they ran back up the stairs again.

"What's going on?" Angela panted. "Is Marian okay?"

"We think Isobel's after her," Lilian said. "We have to find her."

But when they reached the dorm, it was empty. As Lilian looked at it, for a brief, unpleasant moment it felt like a warning.

Four empty beds.

Four missing girls.

"Should we split up?" Serena suggested.

"I don't think so," Lilian said. "Best we stick together.

But she could be anywhere!"

As they stood there, desperately trying to come to a decision, they heard a loud knocking from the wall. All three of them paled and looked at each other.

"That's what I heard on my first night," Angela whispered. "It's Cold Mary!"

"Mary Atkins?" Lilian said, under her breath and then louder. "Mary Atkins?"

Immediately, the knocking stopped.

Lilian walked past Angela's bed and placed her hand against the wall. It felt cold to the touch.

"Mary Atkins, is that you?"

There was silence. About to remove her hand, an almighty thud echoed through the room, making Lilian's palm vibrate.

"Mary, we need your help," Lilian said. "Marian has gone missing and we think she's in danger – from Isobel Boulogne! Do you know where Marian is?"

Again, a brief pause, followed by a knock.

"I can't believe this is happening," Angela whispered.

"I think Mary might be trying to help us," Lilian said. "She was a victim of Isobel, too."

A knock sounded again, this one further away, closer to the doorway.

"I think she wants us to follow her," Lilian cried. "Come on!"

About to dash out, Lilian ran to her bedside drawer and retrieved the necklace. Something told her she might need it. Then they ran out into the corridor, cool air falling on them like a fine rain. A couple of loud knocks came from further down the corridor and they ran towards them.

They waited, straining their ears, not daring to speak in case they missed the next knock.

This time, they heard a distant thud. It took them a moment to realize where it was coming from.

"It's upstairs!" Angela cried.

Lilian pushed her tired legs up one more flight, to the highest floor of the school. There the knocks were louder and more frantic, as if whoever was guiding them wanted them to hurry. Hands pressed to the wall, they shuffled along the corridor until they reached a door marked *FIRE EXIT*.

"She's taking us up to the roof!" Serena gasped. "I can't go any further, you know how I am about heights."

Lilian could see the terror in Serena's eyes.

"It's okay, we can get her," Lilian said. "Stay here and hold the door for us."

She pushed the door open and with Angela in tow, ran up another short flight of stairs and out onto the roof. A blast of cold, October wind gusted into their faces. Leaves scattered down from the inky sky. Dark clouds scudded across a razor-sharp new moon.

And then they saw them.

Two small figures hunched on the edge of the parapet. They were holding hands and looking down towards the ground.

"Maz!" Lilian cried, shouting to make herself heard above the roar of the wind. Keeping one hand on the stone parapet, Lilian edged nearer, closely followed by Angela. Marian turned her head, her black spiky hair tugged by the wind. She frowned, as if confused by what was happening. The figure beside her pulled on her hand, and Lilian saw the other girl. It was another Marian. Just like the not-Angela she'd seen in the library, she was identical to Marian in every respect except for those unnaturally large black eyes.

Both girls looked back down towards the ground, shuffling forward an inch until their toes were right at the edge of the parapet.

Lilian focused her attention on Marian. She could feel hands gripping the bottom of her jumper and knew that

Angela was holding onto her, which gave her confidence to move even closer. Angela shouted something behind her, but the wind snatched her words away. Lilian knew she had to do something.

"Isobel!" she cried. "Isobel Boulogne, we know who you are."

The Marian with the large, black eyes turned and gave Lilian a look of such malevolence that it chilled her bones.

"Isobel," Lilian insisted. "Please let Marian go! She's our friend, and we want her to stay with us."

By way of reply, Isobel's hand tightened on Marian's. Lilian could see the whites of her knuckles. She knew she had only seconds before Marian and Isobel plunged over the side of the roof. Lilian reached into her pocket and grabbed the necklace. She knew Isobel wanted it. It belonged to her sister.

Drawing the necklace out of her pocket, she held it up for Isobel to see.

"Isobel, look! Don't you recognize this?"

Slowly, the other Marian turned and glared at the object. Lilian heard a voice at her shoulder.

"Hey, shipmate, I'll take it from here."

It was Serena. She looked a little green around the gills, but Lilian could see the anger and determination on her face. Marian was her best friend. Grabbing the necklace, Serena opened the clasp, before raising it up high, the silver C turning and catching the moonlight.

"Release our friend and you can have this!" Serena cried. "See? C for Catherine, it's your sister's!"

Instantly, the other Marian began to change. Her features twisted as if in pain, one shoulder hunched up, fingers clenched and unclenched, and Lilian saw the real Isobel appear.

Long red hair. A small mouth that was twisted with anger. And those eyes that resembled something more suited to a nocturnal animal.

Isobel released a dazed-looking Marian and pointed at Serena, eyes flashing with anger.

"You grab Marian while I lead Isobel away," Lilian whispered to Serena. "Give me the necklace back."

Taking the silver chain, Lilian began to back away, hoping that Isobel would be unable to resist following her sister's necklace. Gingerly, she made her way back across the rooftop towards the fire-exit door, all the while waving the necklace for Isobel to see. On the parapet, she could see Serena and Angela stepping slowly towards Marian, who still stood precariously on the edge, swaying like a sapling in a breeze.

At last, Isobel began to follow Lilian, her hunched figure scuttling over the tiles towards her, leaving Marian on the parapet. Serena and Angela rushed in and bundled Marian back to safety. A door opened further down, and Mr Bullen emerged onto the roof, immediately taking everything in with a shocked expression. With a huge surge of relief, Lilian knew that Marian was out of harm's way.

Turning, she fled down the stairs. Now it was Lilian who was in Isobel's sights. All she wanted to do was to get as far away as possible. To lead Isobel away from her friends and the school. She glanced back up the staircase but couldn't see or hear anyone following her.

Had Isobel gone?

Lilian slowed as she descended, not wanting to trip and injure herself. Every few steps she paused, but there was just an eerie silence. She began to wonder if that was the end of it. Maybe, now they'd got Marian back, Isobel had simply given up?

She reached the front doors and opened them. Moonlight streaked the grass. Turning, so she could see anyone coming after her, Lilian backed away across the lawn. The doors to the school slowly swung closed. Lilian stood and watched them, waiting for the handle to turn, her skin like ice as fear rippled through her body. In her hand, she nervously played with the necklace, running its links back and forth through her fingers. It felt like minutes had passed but Lilian couldn't be sure. A bat swooped by her head, making her jump. But nothing came through the doors. She stood alone on the grass, with just the moon and the bats and the owls for company.

Finally, Lilian began to relax. It seemed she was in the clear. Isobel had returned to whichever dark place she came from.

It was then that Lilian felt cold fingers close on the back of her neck.

It was followed by a cracked whisper.

"Give…it…to…me."

Lilian couldn't move. She was rooted to the spot, every strand of hair screaming silently as they stuck up from her scalp. The cold fingers reached down to grasp Lilian's shoulder and squeezed, sending icy tremors rippling through Lilian's body. Then, they began to spin her slowly around.

Lilian turned to see two huge pools of blackness just inches from her face. A mass of red hair framed Isobel's chilling pale features.

"Give…it…to…me," Isobel repeated.

Lilian drew the necklace up with one hand and let it dangle from her fingers, just out of Isobel's reach, the chain catching the light like a silvery flame.

"You want this?"

Isobel nodded once. And then she began to change.

Her head seemed to collapse inwards, as if squashed together by invisible hands. One arm flew out from her body and hung there like a snapped branch. Skin stretched and rippled over bones. And then for one terrible moment, Lilian was looking at herself.

Her fetch.

It was like looking into a mirror, only one whose glass was made of broken shards. Yet there she was. Lilian Jones. A pointy chin. A long nose. A black bobbed haircut. Identical in every respect except that for those huge, horrible eyes.

As Isobel stretched out a hand towards the necklace, Lilian spun out of Isobel's grasp and ran towards the lake. An unearthly screech echoed through the night. Lilian sprinted, not knowing how she was managing to breathe, but refusing to stop. The water lapped at the shoreline, waves rippling like molten silver. Then, Lilian turned, watching what appeared to be her own identical twin stride towards her.

"Here, Isobel, you can have it!" Lilian cried, before flinging the necklace towards the water with all her strength. It looped through the air, a shimmering circle, before landing with a gentle splash.

Isobel ran to the water's edge. Turning, she glared at Lilian.

Then, in an instant, Lilian's likeness fell off Isobel's face like a discarded coat flung to the floor, and Isobel was herself again. Without looking at Lilian, she began to wade out into the water, her bony arms reaching down into the water like fishing nets as she searched. Deeper she sank, the water rising above her waist, the back of her long red hair trailing behind in the water like a scarlet cloak.

And then, underneath the water, Lilian saw something coming towards Isobel.

A shadowy figure swam just inches beneath the surface. Something that wore an identical blue dress to the one Isobel had on. Closer it came, like a crocodile silently hunting its prey.

Isobel saw it and her body trembled. She reached further down beneath the water, holding out her arms as if in welcome. For a moment, something reared out of the water. Lilian saw red hair and a flash of white. Something that could have been bone.

The two figures embraced.

Skeletal arms wrapped themselves around Isobel's back.

Lilian heard Isobel say one last thing.

"My…dear…sister."

Then there was silence.

Before Isobel was dragged below the surface and into the embrace of her sister.

Chapter 17

Lilian struck a match and held it to the candlewick until it caught. She reached for Marian's hand and gave it a squeeze.

"Ready?" she asked.

Marian nodded.

Lilian turned to Angela and Serena, the candlelight casting eerie shadows on their faces.

"Ready?"

They both nodded.

"I'm not scared," Angela said. "Go on."

For once, Lilian believed her.

A week had passed since they'd found Marian on top of the school. Now they were sat in a circle on the floor of their dormitory. Ms Strange had just been in to wish them goodnight. They waited a few minutes until they thought it safe to get out of bed, then they put into action the plan they'd decided on earlier that day. They had someone to thank for helping them escape the clutches of Isobel Boulogne.

Lilian took a deep breath.

"Mary, Mary Atkins," she whispered. "This is Lilian Jones. Are you there?"

Outside, the wind gusted and a cold draught snaked across the dormitory floor, making the girls hunch their shoulders and hold hands even tighter.

"Mary, are you there?" Lilian said again, looking around the room.

There came a quiet tap from the wall behind Angela's bed.

The girls exchanged expectant glances.

"Did you hear that?" Serena whispered.

Lilian nodded and spoke again.

"Hello, Mary. There's someone here who'd like to say something."

The girls all looked at Marian, who gulped.

"Hello, Mary, it's Marian Dawson. I just wanted to say thank you for helping us, for helping me. I don't know how the girls would have found me without you. It was really frightening but I'm fine now. I was worried about my mum – she wasn't very well, and it made me really sad. Lilian thinks that's what attracted Isobel. But the good news is that all my mum's tests came back okay, so I don't have to worry about her any more. She's going to be fine and so are we. But I don't know what we would have done without you."

There was silence for a few moments, before they heard another quiet tap.

Serena cleared her throat. The girls smiled at her. They knew what was coming.

"Hi, Mary, this is Serena Khan. We were wondering, me and the girls here, we're all members of this club. They call us The Midnight Creepers. We're like…um… sisters and get into trouble a lot and do stuff we're not supposed to. But we look after each other, too. And we'd like to invite you to join us. What do you think?"

Another soft tap.

Serena gave them the thumbs up.

"I think that's a yes!"

"And you know, Mary," Lilian said. "Things have settled down here now. Maybe you've been waiting here at Shadowhall because you were worried about other girls being taken by Isobel? If that's the case, then you don't have to worry any more. Isobel has her sister back now and she doesn't need to take anyone else. Everyone's safe and sound."

There was silence again. But after a few moments, Lilian became aware that someone else was in the dormitory with them. Over on Angela's bed, a young girl sat cross-legged, looking at them all. Her silhouette was vague and indistinct, and appeared to shimmer with a soft light, as if a lamp burned somewhere deep within her. Lilian smiled at her. Having been unable to see Mary properly on the school photograph, it felt good to finally get a sense of what she looked like. She had blonde hair, cut into a bob like Lilian's, the sides of which framed her face perfectly. Her eyes were the kind sort, the type that look out on the world with gentleness and curiosity.

Mary smiled and raised a hand.

As one, the girls all waved back. Marian wiped away a tear.

"Thanks, Mary," Lilian said.

Then, before their eyes, like a dying ember, Mary Atkins slowly faded away.

* * *

The next day, the girls gathered in Mr Bullen's office. He'd brought in the painting of Isobel Boulogne for them to look at. Nobody said anything for a while.

"I think the figure in the background is also Isobel Boulogne," Lilian said. "The one with the skull is supposed to be her dark side."

"It's possible," Mr Bullen said.

"I think it's meant to be her sister, Catherine," Marian said. "She has a skull for a face because she died before Isobel."

"That's also possible." Mr Bullen nodded. "All of this is open to interpretation. It's what makes art so fascinating. All of us can look at the same painting and see something different – and we're all right. Fantastic, isn't it?"

"I don't think the girl in the front of the painting is Isobel at all," Angela said, quietly. "It's Catherine. The skull girl in the background is obviously Isobel. Whoever painted this knew exactly what was going on."

Everyone's mouths fell open and they all stared at Angela, who flushed a little with embarrassment.

"Angela wins the *guess-the-meaning-of-the-painting* competition," Serena said, giving Angela a delighted round of applause.

"I hadn't even considered that possibility," Mr Bullen

said. "Perhaps the painting was labelled incorrectly?"

All the girls slowly nodded.

"So, if Catherine drowned in the lake, why wasn't she found at the time?" Angela said, twitching her spectacles with her nose. "Surely they would have searched the lake when she first went missing?"

Mr Bullen turned to her.

"Yes, you would assume that would have been one of the first places they might look. And yet we have no idea how the lake has changed over time. It may have been much deeper than today. Perhaps the lake bed was full of vegetation, the type that might snare and conceal a body. And we must remember that they didn't have the kind of underwater diving equipment we have now."

"I think Isobel knew Catherine might be in the lake," Lilian said. "She tried to get in there to see and maybe that's how she drowned? And then they brought her body back to the house. Perhaps if she'd been left in the lake with Catherine, none of this would have happened?"

"Wonder how her necklace got in our wall?" Serena asked.

Mr Bullen pressed a finger against his cheek.

"Again, we have no way of knowing how the house might have changed over time," he said. "It could have been a bedroom originally?"

"Great," Serena said. "So we're sleeping next to a dead girl's bedroom too!"

"It's sad really," Angela said. "Isobel just wanted her sister back."

"You weren't stood on the edge of the roof with her," Marian said.

Angela blushed.

"Oh, sorry, Maz, I didn't…"

"It's okay, I know what you mean," Marian said. "And you're right, it is sad."

Then they left Mr Bullen to his tea and biscuits.

"Pretty crazy for a first term, eh?" Serena mumbled through a mouthful of pillow when they were back in their dormitory.

"You're not wrong," Lilian said.

It was a few moments before Angela replied, too.

"Apart from the ghost in the wall and being snatched from my bed in the middle of the night, and Marian nearly falling off the roof, I think it's been great!"

Which gave them all a good laugh before one by one, they sank into deep sleeps and sweet dreams.

* * *

The next day was a Sunday, the day Lilian always phoned home. She chatted with her mum for a while before Susan got on the line and Lilian couldn't resist telling her a little about what had happened.

"I'll tell you more when I come home at Christmas," Lilian said.

"But I can't wait that long! You said the school's haunted!" Susan cried, on the other end of the telephone.

"It'll make the perfect Christmas ghost story," Lilian said. "It'll be worth waiting for, I promise."

"Aw, okay," Susan said. "So, it's all back to normal now?"

"Yes, actually, it's pretty boring," Lilian said. "Just lessons and bad food."

"Okay, well, Mum is making *hurry up* faces at me so I'd better say goodbye. Dad's been moaning about the phone bill again."

"Sounds like it's all back to normal there as well," Lilian said. "Okay, talk soon, bye."

"Bye, Lilian!"

As Lilian walked back up the stairs towards the dormitory, she stopped by the wooden banister and gave the two carved lions a pat on the head. Smiling to herself, she could scarcely believe everything that had happened.

But now, the school did seem to have lost some of its more sinister atmosphere. It was still chilly and gloomy, but there were a few girls milling about in the corridors and even Sarah Shoesmith and Sally Baldwin nodded and smiled as they passed.

Lilian was finding her feet, for sure.

As she neared the dormitory, she heard footsteps behind her.

For a second, she felt a cold shiver twist down her spine.

Turning, she saw Ms Strange and Miss Coates walking towards her. One grey figure and one colourful one. They made an interesting pair. They had their heads down and were deep in conversation, so much so that they didn't notice Lilian until they were almost right next to her.

"Good evening, Lilian," Ms Strange said, giving her an awkward smile. "I trust you've recovered from all the excitement?"

"Yes, miss," Lilian said.

"And Marian is none the worse for wear?" Miss Coates asked. "Mr Bullen told us all about her terrifying sleepwalking incident. Imagine getting all the way up to the roof – how awful that could have been!"

Sleepwalking had been their official explanation. It

had raised a few eyebrows but seemed to have been accepted.

"She's fine," Lilian said. "I think it was just a one-off."

"Yes, I'm sure," Ms Strange said, giving Lilian a pointed look. "Though I do wonder how you all knew she'd gone up there."

"We had some help, miss, from one of the girls who'd seen her. She's a friend of ours."

"Indeed," Ms Strange said, giving Lilian a narrow-eyed stare. "Well, please pass on my thanks to her. And Serena and Angela are well, too?"

"They're all fine, miss, everything's fine," Lilian said.

And this time, she meant it. Everything *was* fine. She had three amazing new friends and, best of all, they all got to share a room and swap stories every night. Mary Atkins was at peace, as were Isobel and Catherine Boulogne. At least, Lilian hoped they all were. Mr Bullen had become a friend, too. He'd even told Lilian that he'd noticed how good she was at quickly understanding complicated subjects and wondered whether she might make a good teacher herself one day? Lilian wasn't sure about that. She had plans to go exploring in the Peruvian jungle, but it had still made her feel very proud.

Although it had been terrifying, their supernatural

experience had also been quite thrilling. Lilian doubted that anything as extraordinary as this would ever happen to them again.

Surely not.

Lilian opened the door to the dormitory and began changing into her pyjamas, making sure her school uniform was folded into small, neat little squares before placing it on the correct shelves in her wardrobe.

Everything in its right place.

Just as she liked it.

THE END

Did you survive your first term at
SHADOWHALL ACADEMY?

Turn the page for a sneak peek at
Lilian's next chilling adventure...

It had been about an hour since Ms Strange, the headmistress of Shadowhall Academy, had completed her evening rounds and told the girls it was time for lights out. For a time, the corridors were quiet except the odd groan as wooden floors and walls cooled and yawned. That was before a door to one of the dormitories slowly creaked open. A moment later, a head appeared. It belonged to Lilian Jones, a tall girl with a black bob haircut, a long chin and eyes that normally viewed the world with a quiet, studious curiosity. But tonight, those eyes shone with mischief. She peered left and right, until satisfied that Ms Strange had returned to her room and wasn't lurking in the corridor.

Then, she whispered back over her shoulder.

"Okay, it's all clear."

Dressed in blue striped pyjamas and with thick socks on her feet (perfect for quietening footsteps), she stepped into the corridor. Three other girls followed a second later. Serena Khan came first. She wore stylish purple silk pyjamas, matching slippers and had a long scarlet scarf wrapped around her neck. Her dark hair was tied back into a ponytail and she moved with confident steps and swinging arms, as if she were out for a relaxing stroll. Marian Dawson came next, her choice of nightwear being black pyjama bottoms, black sweatshirt and black socks, which didn't just match her spiky hair, but was her favourite colour for everything, from clothes to nail varnish. Finally, Angela Radford stepped out, a little more hesitant than the other three. Angela wore a thick tartan dressing gown and a bobble hat. She paused for a moment, her eyes wide behind her blue glasses, before gulping. She broke into a run and followed the others. As they passed by certain dormitories, they would pause, before giving the door a quick tap tap with their knuckles. Other doors they ignored. From the doors that they knocked upon, other girls appeared, all following the same practiced routine: a quick glance up and down the corridor, before they began creeping softly down the gloomy corridors of Shadowhall Academy.

They were heading towards the library. During the day, it was a place for reading, or study, or just somewhere quiet where you could look out on the outside world and be alone with your thoughts. Tonight, it was to be different kind of event. Not one that had been officially sanctioned. But Lilian and the other girls tended not to bother about getting official permission. Those little details could be worried about later.

Inside the library, the overhead lights were switched

off and the lamps were turned down low. The curtains were pulled tight against the wind and rain, which tapped and scratched at the windows as if resenting being shut out. Cushions were snatched up. Biscuit tins were prised open. Tea and hot chocolate were passed around, the pleasant warmth of the mugs slowly warming cold hands. Lilian Jones leaned forward in her seat and struck a match, holding it to the candle wick until it caught and began to fizzle softly, casting wisps of white smoke into the air that smelled of vanilla and apple. Then she laid the candle on the table, appreciating the way it cast weird, flickering shadows on to the walls. The atmosphere was perfect.

She glanced to her right, where Serena sat cross-legged on a cushion, her jaw set, her dark eyes shining brightly as if tiny candles burned there, too. Lilian glanced to her right, where Marian and Angela huddled closely together on an old leather sofa, their knees pulled up into their chests with a thick blanket covering them.

It was the first official gathering of the Shadowhall Ghost Story Society.

Look out for the second Shadowhall Academy story, to find out what happens next!